DEBORAH MALONE

CHILLED IN CHATTANOOGA

A TRIXIE MONTGOMERY COZY MYSTERY

A LAMP POST BOOK

CHILLED IN CHATTANOOGA

BY DEBORAH MALONE

ISBN 10: 1-60039-219-9
ISBN 13: 978-1-60039-219-1
ebook ISBN: 978-1-60039-734-9

Copy Edit / Back Cover Copy: Melissa Williams Netherton

www.lamppostpubs.com

CHILLED IN CHATTANOOGA

a Trixie Montgomery cozy mystery

BY DEBORAH MALONE

I pray that out of his glorious riches he may strengthen you with power through his Spirit in your inner being so that Christ may dwell in your hearts through faith.

Ephesians 3:16-17 (NIV)

ACKNOWLEDGEMENTS

First and foremost I want to thank my incredible editor, Beverly Nault. Without Bev's hand to rope in Trixie and the girls no telling what trouble they'd get into.

As always I want to thank my readers. You've encouraged me, inspired me and kept me writing. Without readers there wouldn't be much need for writer's. Keep on reading and remember that I'd love to hear from you. You can contact me at www.deborah-malone.com.

Dedication

Chilled in Chattanooga is dedicated to my friends and family
who have encouraged me throughout my writing journey.
My mother and father didn't get to see me become
a published author, but I know they would have been proud.
I'm thankful for the love of reading they instilled in me.
It was this love of reading that lead to my love of writing.
Thank you Mother and Dad.

CHAPTER ONE

A *body in the deep freeze? Dear God, please help me.*

Harv, my boss at *Georgia by the Way,* gave me grief when I told him I wanted to attend a three day intensive workshop for magazine writers. I finally convinced him it would be for the good of the magazine. I wished I hadn't been so convincing.

Yes, Annie possessed a brash side and rubbed some of the writing students the wrong way, but murder? How could attending an intensive writer's workshop end up in my discovering our teacher's body in the deep freeze?

How in the name of all that's good did I find myself in the vicinity of another dead body? This wasn't the first body I'd found, but I prayed it would be my last. Since I began writing for *Georgia by the Way,* a magazine where past meets present, I'd stumbled into several murder investigations. I cringed at the thought of becoming another Jessica Fletcher.

As I waited my turn for Detective Bianca Sams' interrogation, my mind traveled back a little more than twenty-four hours ago. I needed to make sense of the senseless murder of Annie Henderson. As I journeyed alone in my mind's eye I could see my great-aunt Nana plain as the nose on her face. I heard her call out into the night.

"Would you look at those lights – breathtaking! Oh, there's an elf, take our picture together."

My great-aunt, also known as Nana, gushed over the Enchanted Christmas light display at Rock City on Lookout Mountain, Georgia.

The numerous fairy lights twinkled like a sky full of stars. Nana took off in a slow run. I didn't know such a thing existed until I saw her version of running. Guilt shrouded me for laughing; after all she is a senior citizen. "Nana, wait on us!" In a flash she'd grabbed the arm of an elf mascot and pulled him toward her. The surprised elf pulled the other way, but Nana held on with a death grip.

"Get that camera of yours and start shooting. I want something to remember this night by. You know my memory ain't so good anymore." That might be true, but most of the time Nana's memory rivaled an elephants. I believe the term is selective memory. Many times since I'd moved back home I believed Nana used her age to get away with quirky antics. On our last vacation to Tybee Island, without anyone's knowledge, she decided to get a tattoo "a mermaid to remember our trip by." As if anyone could forget.

I removed my camera from my shoulder, focused and clicked away. Since working for *Georgia by the Way,* I'd taken hundreds of pictures. Harv required photos with his articles, so photography had become second nature to me.

When Nana begged me to come along on this trip, I hesitated. That is, until my best friend Dee Dee Lamont promised she'd come and help me keep herd on Nana. Dee Dee had more patience with Nana than I did. I loved her dearly, but my patience remained in practice mode.

Nana did a 360 and let out a big sigh. "Ain't this something? Just look at all these lights. Have you ever seen anything like it, Trix?" Nana looked at me, eyes wide with excitement, reminding me of a child at Christmas.

I told the truth when I said, "No, I don't believe I have, Nana." The lights at Rock City were nice, but a little too much for me. I preferred the jaw-dropping view from the top of Lookout Mountain. We arrived in time to see the sunset from Lover's Leap, one of the observation points at Rock City. The park boasts that you can see seven states from several points on the grounds. The sunset was God's display of lights and what an exhibition he put on for us. The blue and pink hues merged together, weaving a beautiful tapestry as the orange ball disappeared.

Thinking of Lover's Leap brought bittersweet memories to mind. Time had flown and I'd already been married for almost a year to the most wonderful man, Beau Beaumont. I'd traveled to Chattanooga to attend an intensive workshop for magazine writers. Beau, a deputy sheriff, was in Texas taking classes for recertification. I missed him. This would be the first time we'd been apart for more than a couple of days.

Dee Dee nudged me. "Hey girl, get with the program. If we don't get a move on Nana's going to take that elf home with us."

That put a burr under my saddle. "Come on, Nana. Let's go back to the hotel. This is our last night together before I attend the workshop. Then you and Dee Dee will be on your own for a couple of days." I hugged Nana. "Think you can get along without me?"

Dee Dee and Nana shared a grin. "Sure we can, Trixie," Nana said.

"Well, that makes me feel loved."

"Aw come on, Trixie, don't be such a whiner. You know we love you. But that doesn't mean we can't get along without you." Dee Dee laughed to soften the sting of her comment. "Come on ladies, let's get a move on so we can stop for some hot chocolate at the Café Espresso." We'd booked a hotel room at the Chattanooga Choo Choo and were delighted when we discovered you could stay in an authentic railroad car. I looked forward to a restful night in the Victorian room.

I'd been to the Chattanooga train station before, but it had been years ago. Time had clouded my memory of the beautiful building. When we walked into the historic station the first thing that caught my eye was the multi-colored dome covering the concourse. Four enormous brass chandeliers hung from the ceiling.

We enjoyed a cup of hot cocoa at the little out of the way café and headed to our room. "I don't know about y'all, but I'm ready to hit the hay," Dee Dee said. " I'm going to change into my pajamas and I'll be right out." True to her word, in a few minutes she stepped out of the small bathroom wearing red pajamas covered in black and white kitties decorated with wreaths around their necks. Even though Dee Dee had two grown children of her own, she referred to her five cats as her children.

She stretched and yawned loud enough to wake the dead. "Okay, I'm ready for some shut-eye."

"You and me both girl." I changed into my night clothes while Dee Dee was in the bathroom. I just needed to wash my face.

"Hey, don't go to sleep yet. We have too much to talk about." I looked at Nana decked out in footie pajamas, a far cry from her usual Victoria's Secret nighties. I guess the December weather was too much for her usual nighttime attire. I wondered why she wanted to stay up – we were all tired.

A knock on the door interrupted my thoughts. Nana and I raced to the door. I beat her by a nano-second.

CHAPTER TWO

"Hi," two elves, one male and one female, stood in the hallway and saluted me smartly, "we're here to tuck you in."

"Oh, I'm so sorry. You have the wrong room." I started to shut the door when Nana tugged on my arm.

"Don't go!" Nana yelled. "You have the right room." She pulled them inside and turned toward me. "Surprise! This is for you and Dee Dee. Isn't it the greatest thing since sliced bread?"

Dee Dee, her eyes the size of saucers, stared straight at the pixies. "What in the world?" She turned to Nana. "You did this?"

"Yes, I did. Now you two quit acting like a couple of ole fuddy-duddies and get with the act. I thought this would be a great idea. Trixie, you take yourself way too seriously, so I decided you needed a little laughter in your life."

I looked at Dee Dee and tried to telepath my thoughts. She shrugged as if to say she had no idea Nana planned this *surprise*. I winced at the idea of her capers already starting. Nana was going to be a handful, and I wasn't sure Dee Dee could rein her in. Now that the elves were here I guess there wasn't much to do but acquiesce and endure a tucking-in by a pair of Santa's helpers.

"Okay, Nana, you win. Let's get this over with." I shot Dee Dee a serious look. "That means you too, friend." We endured the next twenty minutes while the elves read us nighttime stories and sang Christmas carols. By the time they left, I'd mellowed quite a bit. Maybe Nana knew more about me than I gave her credit for. Dee Dee assured me we'd laugh about this in the morning. I hoped she was right.

I slept fitfully, dreaming of elves rocking me to sleep as I lay in a giant cradle. Nana popped into the fantasy as an elfette. She kept laughing and saying to the other elves, 'isn't she cute? That's my grandniece.' Then she cackled and disappeared until she made another surprise appearance. Then Dee Dee wound up in the cradle with me donned in her red kitty pajamas. Believe me when I say it was one crowded cradle.

Beau made a grand appearance wearing a suit of armor. He literally lifted me from the cradle and into his arms as he spoke softly in my ear, "Let's go home, honey." When I woke to a room filled with sunlight I sensed someone staring at me. I turned to see Dee Dee propped on her elbow in the next bed. Her hair reminded me of a porcupine in defensive mode. Should I tell her?

"What were you grinning about? Or is it too steamy to tell me?" Dee Dee laughed at her witty comment.

"No, it's not too steamy – not to say I'd tell you if it was. I had this crazy dream about elves and I thought I'd be in their clutches until Beau came and rescued me." I thought how this wasn't far from the truth. A few years ago, my then husband, Wade Middlebrooks Montgomery III, decided to check the grass on the other side of the fence. He found his true love on the internet, and after 20 years of marriage he announced his departure to California to meet the blonde bombshell he'd met in a chat room.

Shortly after he arrived in the sunny state he discovered that all things on the internet are not as they seemed. His soul mate turned out to be a 300 pound bimbo who conned men. He returned to Atlanta with a chip on his shoulder and a destroyed marriage.

Left with a bankrupt heart and an empty bank account I ran home to Mama with my tail between my legs. She took me under her wings and helped me through the difficult times.

Dee Dee wore a sweet smile. "Isn't it amazing how our dreams replicate real life? Beau is a real life knight in shining armor and you are one lucky damsel in distress."

Nana's gray head popped up from across the room. "You got that right. If I'd been just a few years younger I'd have given you a run for your money."

"A few years, Nana?" I loved to tease my great-aunt. Since moving back to Vans Valley, Nana and I had formed a bond. When Mama was young she lost both parents. Nana, her mother's sister, stepped in and raised her like her own. When Nana's husband died and she nose-dived into a deep depression, Mama insisted she move in with her.

Mama quickly discovered Nana's personality had changed as she'd grown older. She used to be prim and proper and would never draw attention to herself. Now Nana's behavior had put Mama in a tizzy more than once. Mama thought she might have the beginnings of Alzheimer's, but I'd decided Nana knows exactly what she's doing and uses her age to get away with her outrageous antics.

Albeit, it still took the patience of Job to be with Nana any length of time. Mama and I took turns keeping an eye on her. I didn't mind bringing her along on my trips to give Mama a rest, as long as I had Dee Dee to help.

"Hmph, watch it Missy," Nana's endearment for me when she meant business.

"Come on, let's go find something to eat. I just need a little something, I'm not very hungry."

Dee Dee and I exchanged knowing glances. Nana usually ate like a dog with worms and could give a grown man a run for his money. But, according to her, she ate like a bird. I agreed, since a bird eats all the time.

Dee Dee placed her arm around Nana's shoulder and pulled her close. "I'm with you Nana. My stomach is yelling 'feed me, feed me.' She turned toward me. "Trix, have any ideas where we should eat."

"I don't think I'll eat with y'all this morning. They'll be serving breakfast pastries at the workshop. I'd better get going if I don't want to be late." I felt bad leaving Dee Dee with the responsibility of watching Nana, but she assured me they'd be fine.

The Chattanooga Choo Choo is located downtown, so the drive

to the workshop wasn't far. At the end of Main Street I could see the unique glass building that housed the Aquarium. It stood high above the skyline like a sentinel guarding the historic city. I took a right on Third and then turned onto High Street leading to the artsy area known as the Bluff View Art District. The streets wove through the hills of the quaint area. A young couple on bicycles rode past me.

A charming bed and breakfast had been chosen for the workshop venue. I looked forward to learning as much as I could about magazine writing. More than two years had passed since I'd started working for Harv, and I'd learned a lot on the job, but I was eager to expand my knowledge. I knew Beau would take care of me, but memories of being without money haunted me.

My phone played a jaunty melody. I answered it, expecting Harv to be the caller.

"Hi Sweetie, you got there yet. How is it?"

I released a big sigh. Nana! "No I'm not there yet, I'm still looking for the right house. I've got to go Nana. I can't talk and look, too." Ever since Nana had acquired a phone for seniors, sporting large numbers and speed dial, she jumped at any chance to make a call. More often than not I was the recipient.

"Okie dokie, be sure and let us know when you get checked in and scope out your room. I want to hear all about it. Dee Dee and I are on our way to look at Christmas decorations. We might even ride the Duck." I couldn't imagine Nana riding on the Duck, an apparatus that looked like an army tank that went from riding on wheels to floating on the river. But then she's surprised me more than once.

"Okay, have a good time and I love you," I said.

"Love you, too. Now don't get into any trouble."

We hung up and I returned to the task of finding the venue for the workshop. We planned to spend the night so we could have late classes and get up early and start all over. Talk about intensive! I already knew there were several bed and breakfasts in the Bluff District. The District itself is small and encompasses only a couple of blocks. As I intently surveyed my surroundings I spotted a Victorian era house. The sign in front read The James R. Jones House, Bed and Breakfast. That was it! I slammed on my brakes and backed up since I'd passed the narrow driveway.

I didn't know a lot about architecture, but I knew enough to label it Edwardian. A number of steps led to the porch. A porch, the length of the house and dotted with white wicker chairs, invited the stranger to come and sit a spell. The second floor possessed a balcony and large, elongated, curved-top windows decorated the front. It boasted a cupola on top opening onto a balcony.

As I sat in the driveway, my PT Cruiser idling, I surveyed the myriad of trees and bushes spread around the small front yard. Since it was December, and most of the plants were bare, it leant an eerie feel to the portly old house. The hair on the back of my neck stood at attention and a chill ran up my spine. My heart beat rapidly for just a minute, but then I shook off the ominous feeling. I chuckled out loud and scolded myself. *For goodness sake, what can happen at a writer's workshop? Probably just the excitement, like a girl feels on the first day of school, right?*

CHAPTER THREE

A horn blared and jarred me from my musings. I looked around to study the offending car behind me. Guess they wanted to use the driveway, too. I drove around to the back of the house where a small gravel parking lot greeted me.

I'd wait to carry in my luggage. The proud owner of a new knee, I wanted to see what challenges I faced first. Playing sports and being thrown from a horse named Grace had damaged my original knee beyond repair requiring a total replacement this past year.

A little red sports car pulled into the space beside me. A pair of the longest legs I'd ever seen slid out of the little car. How they fit in the tiny car was a mystery. The elongated limbs were attached to a middle-aged redheaded woman.

I took the initiative and introduced myself. "Hi, I'm Trixie Beaumont." She looked at my extended hand like it was covered with warts. I withdrew it.

"Hi." She marched past me, into the house. I wondered if she'd signed up for the workshop. If everyone possessed her charming personality we were in for a wild ride.

"Hello, you must be Trixie Beaumont." I was pleasantly surprised when an older woman greeted me with a hearty welcome. She grabbed me by the arm and pulled me inside. "Come in, come in." She shut the door behind us.

"Okay, I give up. How did you know my name?"

"Well, dear, you're the last participant to arrive. It was just a matter of elimination. Now that I know who you are I'll return the favor. I'm Annie Henderson, the workshop director. It's good to meet you." She grabbed my hand and pumped it up and down.

"Who was the friendly red-head that breezed in before me? Is she a member of the workshop?" Annie confirmed my worst fear.

"Yes, she sure is. That, my dear, is Tippi Colston." She pointed to a table set up with pastries and a pot of coffee. "Help yourself. When you get through, I'll show you to your room. Our first class will start at nine," her smile disappeared, "and don't be late."

My room exuded charm. A double bed with a canopy would be a welcome sight at the end of the day. An antique chifferobe stood in the corner of the room, in place of a closet. I would have to use the vintage piece of furniture to store my clothes. An antique wash bowl and pitcher sat atop a tall dresser. A full length mirror framed in cherry wood inhabited another corner of the room. I imagined I'd been transported back to a simpler time. There were times in our age of hustle and bustle that I yearned for a time when life moved at a slower pace.

I looked at my watch. I'd better hurry if I didn't want Annie to get upset on our first day. So much for a slower pace. I descended the steep steps as fast as my knee allowed. Some of the participants had already taken their seats, while others talked among themselves. I found a chair and scooted up to a round table.

Annie cleared her throat and looked at us over half-glasses. "Everyone take a seat please."

I acquired a quick head count – six including Annie. I looked around the table at an eclectic group of writers. Three women and two men made up the class, four women including me. The men were outnumbered. I realized I'd be spending the next few days with these people. Everyone looked amicable enough, but I'd learned the hard way, looks could be deceiving.

"Let's go around the table and offer introductions," Annie said. "Start with Trixie and go to the right."

I introduced myself and relinquished the floor to a scruffy looking character sitting beside me.

"Hi there! I'm Bodene Tate, and I plan on making a lot of money telling my jailhouse story." He pushed his shirt sleeves up revealing a myriad of tattoos. "I ain't never wrote nothin', but it can't be that hard. I'm here to learn how to write, so I can tell the world I didn't kill nobody." All eyes turned to the burley parolee.

Annie appeared to have swallowed her tongue. She coughed a few times then begged the next person to continue. I'd noticed the young woman, who had the pleasure to sit on the other side of Bodene, when I entered the room. With her mocha colored skin, short spiked hair, and a tall, slender body, she held the air of an exotic creature. She stood erect with the poise of a dancer. She struck me as someone who possessed self-assurance.

"Good morning. I'm Lori Wilson and I'm editor and contributor for the *Tennessean,* an ad driven magazine that we offer free to the public. My goal is to someday be on the staff of a major women's magazine."

Annie had finally found her voice. "Thank you, Lori. Do I know you from somewhere? You look familiar." She scrunched up her face and tapped her finger on her chin.

"No ma'am. I don't think we've met before." Lori stared straight at Annie and held her gaze. I saw the wheels churning. Annie might not know Lori, but I had no doubt Lori knew Annie.

Lori looked to her right, relinquishing her turn to the next person. It was the gorgeous red-head that brushed me off in the parking lot. Envy's a dangerous emotion, but I had to admit I was jealous of this woman's looks. But then again, I remembered when Mama always said "pretty is as pretty does." Time would tell if she was as pretty as all that.

When she opened her mouth, I swear she sounded like a *valley girl.* "Hi. I'm Tippi Colston – Tippi 'with-an-i.' I'm free-lancing right now with the hopes of owning my own magazine. I don't think I'd be happy working for anyone. I'm used to being my own boss." Tippi "with- an-i" looked around the room as if she dared anyone to disagree with her.

"I'm not sure if there's anything new I can learn, but I thought it would be a nice vacation for a few days."

A Cheshire Cat grin spread across Annie's face. I suspected Annie saw Tippi as a challenge, and somehow I didn't think this would be a vacation. I for one, looked forward to wrapping my mind around Annie's lessons. It would be a break from the article Harv had recently assigned me. The subject was an unsolved murder case that occurred on Lookout Mountain.

Harv wanted me to work on the article while this close to the small Georgia town, but I didn't know how I was going to make time. I brought along my research as well as pictures I'd acquired from people I'd interviewed. I had a lot of organizing to do. I'd have to find a way to squeeze in some work to meet the deadline Harv had set for me.

The next person on Tippi's right introduced himself as George Buchanan. I pegged him to be in his late twenties or early thirties. He sported curly brown hair and the thickest eyebrows I'd ever seen. His face was pock-marked, probably from a severe case of acne when he was a teenager. I couldn't imagine the teasing he endured from fellow classmates.

George informed us he worked for the Rossville Express reporting the arrests, divorces, and things you wouldn't want others to know about your life. His aspiration was to be a photo-journalist for a newspaper or magazine. I was glad to hear he didn't want to be stuck reporting the misfortune of others.

The last introduction was Amanda Holbrook. Amanda had short, blonde hair and was a little heavy-handed on the makeup. Kind of reminded me of Tammy Faye. Even with the hefty amount of makeup she was an attractive lady.

"I'm here because my low-down, no good, cheatin' husband left me high and dry. You wouldn't think your best friend would stab you in the back, but she did. I've been writing for pleasure several years and now it's time to get serious if I want to find a good job. That's all I've got to say."

Humm, seems Amanda and I had a lot in common. I thought I'd

seek her out when I had a chance and offer her a shoulder to cry on. I remembered how devastated I was when Wade left me and how comforting a kind word could be. Anyway, I figured after I told her what Wade did, she'd know she wasn't the only one who had a low-down, no good, cheatin' ex-husband.

Annie put us to work faster than a hound dog on the trail of a coon. She started by asking the class to write an article about a hobby we enjoyed. She took up the assignment and then distributed some hand-outs.

"I'm going to read your papers and then give suggestions," she told us. "After I've given my opinions, feel free to offer ideas to your fellow writers." She had quite a few thoughts on each article letting us know we all had room for improvement. Her lecturing wasn't too bad until she reached George's paper.

She looked over her half-glasses and began her spiel, "Now, here is how not to write an article." She held up George's effort and read it out loud. My face grew hot and I resisted the urge to crawl under the table and it wasn't even my paper. I couldn't begin to imagine how George felt. One look at him and I knew he was beyond embarrassed. He'd moved right into furious. His eyes narrowed and I thought I saw smoke coming from his ears.

When I thought it couldn't get worse – it did. Annie took the offending paper and tore it in two. There was a collective gasp around the table. All eyes went from Annie to George. He sat stunned for a minute and then his chair shot back, scraping the wooden floor as he stood. He grabbed his papers and notebook and stormed out of the room.

CHAPTER FOUR

A fly would've had a grand ole' time with the five mouths that stood agape. I assumed Annie would dismiss the class so she could make amends with George. It wouldn't be the first time, nor the last, that I was sorely mistaken.

Annie proceeded without a hiccup. "Class, let's continue with our next assignment." We closed our mouths, and got back into the zone. We spent the rest of the day working on new assignments. For our last project of the day, Annie suggested we work on a topic we'd normally write about for work. What a break. I could combine my article for Harv with Annie's assignment.

I retired to my room and ached to snooze for a while, but with Harv holding me to a deadline I decided to work on my article. I reviewed the pictures given to me by people I'd interviewed concerning the murder of Mr. Bobby Lee Ghoston. This was not an old murder – well not in the sense of historic. I don't know what it is with Harv, but since I'd been working for *Georgia by the Way*, and unwittingly became involved in three previous murders, he had become fascinated with murder and mayhem. More often than not, murder was my assignment.

I didn't mind so much, I sort of fancied myself an amateur detective now. Bobby Lee Ghoston was a well-known bootlegger and was rumored to be a member of the Dixie mafia. I decided to run my ideas by Annie. I gathered my research and headed to her room.

I passed Tippi "with- an- i" in the hallway outside Annie's room. I

.s determined to speak to her. "Hi, I'm Trixie," I said extending my hand. "I hope we can get to know each other better in the next few days."

Her features didn't soften like I'd expected. "I know who you are. You're that lady who helped solve crimes in Marietta and Tybee Island. You think you're something and I bet you're dying to be the teacher's pet."

Oh my goodness. Did she just say teacher's pet? "Uh, no. Not really."

"I should offer you the professional courtesy to know I wouldn't mind working for *Georgia by the Way* myself. I've already sent in several manuscripts for consideration and I expect to hear back from Harv any time." She stopped just long enough to get her breath.

"You might have robbed me from winning an award at the Excellence Awards last year with your sensational story, but it won't happen again. I have my eye on your job and I intend to do anything it takes to get it."

She stared straight into my eyes. It was hard not to be intimidated, but I'd grown in confidence over the past few years thanks to my faith in God and a bit of trial by fire. I stared back. I expected her to back off but she didn't. I realized how ridiculous we must look and gave in.

"I'm sorry you feel that way Tippi. I'd like to be your friend, but it takes two to tango and I guess you don't want to dance. If you'll excuse me I need to meet with Annie."

Tippi raised her chin a little higher and left me to wonder what hit me.

Annie's room was a little bigger than mine. I guess a perk for being the teacher. Her room was filled with antiques making it a cozy nook. Night had already fallen and she'd turned on a floor lamp beside a Queen Anne wingback chair. Shadows danced on the walls.

"Come in, come in. How might I help you tonight?" She sipped from a cup of hot tea. "Oh, excuse my bad manners. Would you like a cup of Rose Petal Green Tea? It's one of my indulgences so to speak. I can only find it one place on the internet, but the soothing taste is worth it."

Annie took a sip. "Ummm, good. Would you be a dear and set this on the dresser by the teapot?" I didn't mind since I was closer. I reached for the delicate cup and placed it beside the tea canister decorated in flowers. I picked up the pretty container and admired the handiwork. The entire set matched.

"My mother gave that set to me and her mother gave it to her. It's been in the family for years." She sat up a little straighter in her chair and gave me her full attention. "Now, let's talk about you."

"I'm working on an article for *Georgia by the Way,* and I wanted your opinion on combining it with the article I need to write for you. It's about an unsolved murder that happened on Lookout Mountain. I have some pictures and I'd like you to look at them."

"Yes, it'll be fine to combine the two. I sure hope the remainder of our time improves the writing of my students." Annie's voice became louder as she ruminated about the assignments. "I tell you, I've never seen such sloppy writing."

A knock at the door interrupted Annie's tirade. "Come in."

"Ms. Henderson?" The door slowly opened. "I'm Ladonna. Here are some extra towels I thought you might like." Ladonna's lovely mocha complexion was highlighted by a lovely smile until she saw me. "To be honest, I thought you sounded upset as I passed by in the hallway."

She looked at me accusingly, then offered a show of concern to Annie.

"It's quite all right," Annie said. "We were just talking shop, but now that you mention it, I'm not feeling well. My stomach is killing me."

CHAPTER FIVE

Annie clutched her stomach. "Trixie, I think I'm going to have to cut our meeting short. I don't feel up to company right now." In a few minutes, her face had turned from a healthy pink to the white of a new fallen snow.

"Is there anything I can do for you Ms. Henderson?" Ladonna looked as worried as I felt.

"Annie, I'd be glad to sit with you for a while." I didn't mind staying if she needed me. "Perhaps we should call a doctor."

"No, no you girls go on. I'd rather be by myself, I'm a private person. I'm just going to lie down for a while."

I returned to my room, worried about her. She'd turned ill so suddenly. An ulcer perhaps? She did seem pretty tightly wound.

I wanted to get to my article, but first things, first. I should call Nana and Dee Dee and see how they fared all day. If I knew Nana, and I knew Nana, she'd run Dee Dee ragged.

Dee Dee answered on the second ring. "Hey Trix, how ya' doing? Getting much done?"

I could hear Nana in the background begging Dee Dee to hand her the phone. "I haven't done much yet, but I plan on putting the pedal to the metal tonight. Remember that unsolved murder on Lookout Mountain I told you about?"

"The one about Mr. Ghoston?"

"That's the one. Well, our teacher told me I could work on it for tomorrow's assignment. I'm itching to get on it. I need to study the photos and separate them into categories." I could see Nana in my mind's eye jumping up and down with anticipated excitement of telling me about their day's adventure. "Let me speak to Nana before she loses her knickers."

"Okay, but I want to talk with you before you hang up."

The next voice I heard belonged to a little lady I'd come to dearly love over the past few years. "Hey, Trixie. You aren't going to believe all we did today." If it involved Nana, I'd believe it. "We went to the Chattanooga Aquarium. I've never seen so many fish in all my life."

"That's great, Nana."

"Wait a minute, honey. I'm not through. Then we rode the Duck. I've never had so much fun. I can't wait until tomorrow. I want to go on a carriage ride and maybe visit the History Museum."

I was exhausted just listening to Nana's itinerary. We talked a few more minutes as she told me about her eventful day. *God love Dee Dee.* When I came back to Vans Valley after Wade's little tryst, lower than a snake's belly, I couldn't see how I would ever regain my self-esteem. Not only that, I'd acquired a large chip on my shoulder that grew every day as I continued to add bitterness to it until it felt like a boulder. The one thing that bothered me the most was the hit my faith took. I was one sorry mess.

An angel, in the form of Dee Dee Lamont, came to my rescue. As soon as she found out I'd returned home, she insisted we renew our friendship where we'd left off in high school. Dee Dee was no stranger to pain. Her husband, Gary, had died a year earlier of a sudden heart attack. Her faith and strength were an example I strived to follow. With her guidance I not only regained my self-esteem, but my faith grew stronger and stronger. Yes, I still dealt with old doubts and bitterness sometimes, but I found it a lot easier to recover from those bouts of doubt and uncertainty. I hoped I could be as good a friend to Dee Dee.

"That's wonderful, Nana. Could I speak to Dee Dee again? I need to get back to work."

"You sure can. Sorry you're missing all the fun, but maybe you can join us later." A cackle came through the phone. She didn't sound upset over my absence.

"Hey, Trixie. I guess Nana filled you in."

"She sure did. How in the world did you keep up with her? She has more energy than a grasshopper on steroids." I couldn't wait to give Dee a big hug for her help.

"It wasn't easy, but I managed. I'm just glad we're back in our room to take a break for the rest of the day. I'm so tired I wouldn't even mind if the elves tucked me in tonight." Dee Dee never failed to produce a laugh from me. "Your mama is a saint. I don't know how she does it day after day."

"I always say she's a direct decedent of Job. I guess I need to go and get busy on my article. I hope you get a good night's rest and Nana doesn't pull any of her stunts tomorrow."

"Night, Trix."

I worked on my manuscript until my eyes crossed and then crawled into bed, grateful for the cool, dark room and firm mattress.

Sleep came quickly, but a growling stomach woke me up. The digital clock read 3:45a.m.

I tried to go back to sleep without much success. I gave up and slipped into my robe and slippers, and headed downstairs to find something to satisfy the hungry beast within. I cat walked downstairs hoping I wouldn't wake anyone.

Moonlight shone through the window enough for me to find the light switch. When I flipped the switch, light flooded the kitchen. I headed to the industrial-sized stainless steel refrigerator and found some cheese and grapes. Popping in a juicy red seedless, something odd caught my eye. A length of fabric hung out of the freezer door. Worried the compromised seal would spoil the perishables inside; I opened the freezer to see a pink length of fabric, like a sash, that had gotten caught in the door.

It wasn't the sash that stole my breath away. What laid me flat on the floor was the body attached to the other end.

CHAPTER SIX

"Ms. Beaumont." The recognition of my name transported me back to the present.

Detective Biance Sams mirrored Dee Dee's image with the exception of her dark brown skin. I'd met several detectives recently, but she was the first female. This could be a good thing – or not. "If you'll please follow me, we'll get started with your interview."

She led me to a quiet office, grabbed a swivel chair and sat down across from me. Detective Sams possessed the same scrutinizing stare that was common among investigators – a mind-numbing gaze that urged you to confess to a crime whether you were guilty or not. "Now, tell me the sequence of events that led you to find Annie Henderson."

I relayed how I'd gone to meet with Annie and encountered Tippi "with-an-i" outside of Annie's door. Then I talked with Annie about combining my article from work with the article we were to write for her. She told me it would be fine and then Ladonna, the housekeeper, brought some towels in for Annie. Then she told us her stomach was killing her and asked that we leave her alone so she could lie down. *Boy, she wasn't kidding when she said her stomach was killing her.* I stopped to take a breath.

Detective Sams looked a little dazed when I finally slowed down. "That's fine, Trixie. Now tell me why you went downstairs." She straightened up in the chair, accentuating her full-figured body. Hers was a formidable presence.

I told her I wasn't able to sleep very well, and went down looking for something sweet – maybe ice-cream or popsicles. I looked at the Detective, "You know how that is. Don't you?"

She got this far-away look in her eyes like Dee Dee does when we discuss chocolate. "Yes, I sure do." She suddenly seemed to realize we weren't here to deliberate sweets. She cleared her throat and her eyes snapped back to the present. "Okay, let's get back to the freezer."

I told her about the sash, and then the image of Annie lying crumpled in the small freezer was more than I wanted to remember. I felt light-headed, nauseous and then it became more difficult for me to breath. I heard a distant voice say, "I'll be right back."

Next thing I knew I was breathing into a brown paper bag. My breaths became slower and my head didn't feel like it was going to explode. When my thoughts became clearer than mud I saw Detective Sams, about six inches from my face, looking at me with maternal concern. Maybe that was a good sign.

"Feeling better, Trixie?"

"Yes, I am. Thank you."

The detective flipped her notebook closed, "I have what I need for now." She replaced her pen in her pocket and said, "Let's go back and meet with the others. I have a few things I need to discuss with the group."

We met in the sitting room. Someone had lovingly furnished this bed and breakfast with antiques: a roll top desk, wingback chairs, leather sofa, and a fireplace with a clock sitting on the mantle. I wished I could enjoy my surroundings, but that wasn't going to happen right now.

I looked around. Bodene stood by the fireplace, flanked by Tippi and George Buchanan in wingback chairs. Lori sat on the couch and Ladonna stood in front of the fire warming her hands. I was relieved to see an empty chair and headed straight toward it. Detective Sams entered the room behind me. "We're waiting on one more person," she said.

"Everyone needs to listen real close to what I have to say." She surveyed the room, eyeing each of us to make her point. "For those of you who haven't met him, this is Sergeant Gary Sargent."

I guess my nerves got the best of me and I laughed out loud. Everyone stared at me.

Especially Sergeant Sargent. "Ms. Beaumont." Suddenly I went from Trixie, to Ms. Beaumont. "If you've settled down now, I'll continue.

"We are considering this a murder and I'm asking – no telling you – that you must remain in town for the next several days while we continue our investigation."

Oh my goodness! What is Beau going to say? The first time I'm away from Beau since we'd been married and I discover a dead body. The nerves cranked up and a little laugh tried to escape. I fought it back. Fairly sure Detective Sams wouldn't appreciate another interruption, I put my hand over my mouth to control any outbursts.

The detective wasn't finished. "I want all of you to give your personal information to," she looked directly at me before saying, "Sergeant Sargent. I need you to make other arrangements for the night, but you can come and go, as long as you are in touch by cell phone. The crime scene is off-limits for the rest of the day while we investigate. You're dismissed." I stood up, ready to make my escape, so I could call and check on Dee Dee and Nana. Then the detective pulled another rabbit out of her hat. "That is except for Ms. Beaumont."

CHAPTER SEVEN

O*h boy, I'm in trouble now.* "Detective Sams, I've told you all I know." I had the urge to hide under a piece of furniture. Life could be overwhelming at times and surely finding a frozen body would qualify as one of those.

This couldn't be happening to me. I thought when I married Beau life would be beautiful and full of happy endings. I guess just because you're in love doesn't mean you'll be without trials. That thought triggered an example of a Christian life. It doesn't mean we won't have trials, it means we'll have the strength we need available to face our challenges head-on and come out smelling like scented laundry detergent.

"Let's go back in the office, Trixie." The detective's voice shook me back to the present. "I have some information I want to share with you." I followed her back into the same room we'd been in a few minutes earlier. "It seems you were the last person to see Annie Henderson alive. Ladonna told me she heard raised voices coming from behind closed doors and when she knocked, you were in the room with Ms. Henderson."

"Yes, but..."

She motioned me to wait. "I'm not finished yet. And you discovered the body. This doesn't look good for you. We still have the crime scene to investigate, and more questioning to do, but I'm letting you know you need to stay close by in case I need you." She looked directly in my eyes and lowered her voice, "Do you understand?"

"Yes, ma'am, but I want to explain."

"You'll have enough time to explain later. The sergeant or I will be meeting with you again as well as the other guests. You have my word we'll leave no stone unturned. If you're not guilty then you don't have anything to worry about."

Yeah, sure. Easy enough for you to say.

Detective Sams stood directly in front of me. "I'll have Sergeant Sargent accompany you to your room so you can grab a few things. Please leave your information with him and when you find out where you'll be staying be sure and let us know."

"Okay." I swallowed a lump in my throat. After the sergeant left I hurried to my car so I could have some privacy to call someone who loved me. I longed to call Beau, but I knew he couldn't drop what he was doing and run to my rescue.

My best friend picked up in two rings. "Hello."

"Oh, Dee Dee." I stifled a sob.

"What's the matter, girl?"

I managed my next words through a veil of tears. "You're not going to believe what happened."

"What did ya' do? Wait, let me guess, you found a dead body." Raucous laughter shot through the phone.

Dead silence filled the air waves. "Oh – my – goodness. You did find a dead body. Trixie I'm so sorry. Where are you? We'll come pick you up."

I heard Nana in the background, begging Dee Dee to tell her what happened. Guilt riddled my thoughts. I loved Nana dearly, but I didn't know how I was going to get through this and deal with Nana, too. I knew once she heard about the murder she'd want to get involved.

Detective Sams appeared to be capable of doing her job without my help. I had no desire to get involved, but I knew that once my editor, Harv, found out I'd discovered another corpse he'd insist I cover the story. Harv's fascination with murder and mayhem guaranteed I'd become *Georgia by the Way's* police reporter by default before long. I shuddered.

The gray day matched my mood. The bed and breakfast that had appeared stately, now seemed forlorn – a place destined to host death. I waited anxiously for Dee Dee and Nana to show up until they zipped up in a green Ford Fiesta. The little car stuck out like a lime in a basket of lemons.

Dee Dee exited the little car and scooted inside the passenger side of my P.T. Cruiser. "Brrr, it's cold enough out there to make a snowman shiver." She slammed the door and looked at me with her brown hang dog eyes. "Oh, Trixie, I'm so sorry. Come get in my car, it's already warmed up, and you can tell us all about it." She grabbed my camera and pocketbook, "Is there anything else you need?"

"No, I can come back later for more things. Where in the world did you get that car?"

"Don't worry, the color grows on ya'. It was the only one left at the rental place. You ought to see all the looks thrown our way. Nana loves it – she waves at all the men, but I'm not sure if they're seeing her or wondering if we're advertising Vlasic pickles. Knowing Nana she probably thinks they're staring at her. I didn't tell her any different." Dee Dee offered me a silly grin. I appreciated the attempt to cheer me up.

Nana sat in the front seat, so I slid into the back. My knee ached, so I gave it a brisk rub. The cold didn't help. Nana turned around, and called me her pet name that drew more tears. "Sugah, I'm sorry this happened. Now tell us what we need to do." Because we'd helped solve three previous murders, Nana had bragged to her friends that now we qualified as full-blown detectives. "Start from the beginning and don't leave anything out."

"How about we go get something to eat first? I haven't had anything since last night. I could eat a bear."

"Are you up for Sticky Fingers?" Dee Dee threw the pickle-mobile into gear.

"I'm not very hungry, but I'm sure I could eat a little," Nana said.

"I think she was asking me, Nana." When it came to food, Nana could out eat both of us.

We drove through beautiful downtown Chattanooga toward Broad

Street. The historic buildings stood towering over the city. Even though it was a cold day, tourists strolled the sidewalks of downtown. We were lucky to find a parallel parking space close to the famous restaurant.

Couples holding hands, and families bundled in coats and scarves wove in and out of the various stores and restaurants. Children held treasures they had acquired from the gift shops that lined the streets. I turned my head at the clip-clop of hooves on pavement to see a horse drawn carriage with a young couple snuggling in the back seat. The pit of my stomach felt emptier; my distance from Beau greater than before. Yes, I was hungry, but this ache came from missing Beau.

"Ugh!" I bumped into someone as solid as a bear.

"Hey, why don't you watch where you're going," yelled my victim.

"Oh, I'm so sorry. I didn't mean to run into you." His eyes shot daggers at me.

"Well, he didn't have to be so rude," Dee Dee said.

Nana grabbed my elbow. "Let's get off the street where you're a menace and find out why you keep turning up dead people."

Heads turned at her remark, and we hastily entered the restaurant behind a family with four small children. They were having a little trouble keeping the active youngsters in tow.

The hostess approached. "How many please?"

"Three. How long is the wait?"

The young girl awarded us with a broad smile revealing a set of shiny braces. "You won't have to wait at all." She grabbed three menus and packs of tableware and motioned for us to follow her. "Come this way. Your waitress will be Jenny. Could I take your drink order while you wait?" It was unanimous. Sweet iced tea all the way around.

After she left, Nana leaned in conspiratorially. All right, Missy, tell us all about the murder."

I agonized over how much to tell Nana. I knew she'd want to get involved when she found out what happened. I started to relay my story when Jenny, our waitress, approached.

"Ready to order?" We weren't, but we opened our menus and hurriedly picked out what we wanted. We decided on the $7.99 menu. Nana opted for a bowl of Brunswick stew and half a turkey sandwich. Dee Dee ordered a barbeque sandwich and I chose the brisket sliders. As soon as Jenny left, I started to tell my story again when a phone shrilled. We scrounged through our pocketbooks in unison. I was the winner.

I read the caller I.D. with trepidation. "Harv?"

CHAPTER EIGHT

"You've got that right, Kiddo." A booming voice emanated from the phone. "What's going on in the town of Chattanooga? How's the article coming?"

"Whoa, Harv. Look, I can't talk right now; I'm in a restaurant. I'll call you back as soon as I can." I pictured my boss at his desk sucking on a cherry Tootsie Pop. After a scare with his ticker, he'd traded in his ever-present cigars for the sweet treat. I rarely saw Harv at the office without the new vice.

"Okay, but don't take too long. I want an update of that murder story you're working on. Just because you're at a writer's conference doesn't mean you can slack up on your work." I'd found early on that Harv was a sheep in wolf's clothing. His size alone could be intimidating, let alone his booming voice. But underneath the gruff exterior was a heart of gold. He gave this rookie a chance when no one else would. Yes, he expected my best, but I knew he'd look out for me.

"I promise I'll call you later." I knew when Harv found out I'd discovered a dead body he would jump on the story like a dog on a biscuit. We said our goodbyes and I hung up. With the help of another server, Jenny brought out our food and placed it on the table. The next few minutes were quiet, except for the licking of fingers and the smacking of lips.

When we'd eaten enough to satiate our appetites, Nana probed me again about my harrowing experience. "Spill the beans, Missy."

I took a long swig of sweet tea, then wiped my mouth. "Oh, Nana, it was terrible. I got hungry during the night, so I ventured downstairs to find a snack. I noticed what looked like a sash hanging out of the deep freeze. Of course, I opened it. You know what they say..."

"Nothing more than a corps-ical in the middle of the night?" Nana quipped. Her snark broke the tension. Heads turned as laughter rang from our table.

Her gallows humor actually helped me recall the details with more clarity. "Anyway, I opened the lid and there was Annie Henderson surrounded by ice cream and frozen vegetables."

"Oh, Trixie," Dee Dee leaned over and hugged me, "how awful for you. I'm sorry I wasn't there to comfort you. What happened after you found the body?" Dee Dee poised her fork ready to take another bite of potato salad while I explained.

"Detective Bianca Sams showed up, as well as her assistant Sergeant Gary Sargent." Grins broke out on Nana and Dee Dee. "Before y'all say anything, I know it's a funny name, but be careful. She's very protective of her Sergeant Sargent." I stifled a giggle.

"Anyway, she questioned some of us and the sergeant questioned the others. The process seemed routine until Detective Sams asked me to wait after the others had left."

"What did she want with you, Trixie?" Nana tried to scrape more stew from an empty bowl.

Nana wasn't the only one with a healthy appetite. I finished off my sliders, and wondered how I could eat at a time like this. But no matter how dire the circumstances in our life, we still had to eat.

"She said that the house staff, Ladonna, heard Annie and me arguing. We weren't though. Annie was talking and she got louder and louder – it wasn't arguing. I guess it seemed that way to her. Anyway, the detective asked us to stay in town. They're working on the crime scene, so we can't go back to spend the night. I guess you girls are stuck with me."

The waitress walked up and refilled our tea glasses. "Could I get you ladies a dessert?" It was a unanimous "yes." After much discussion we decided on homemade bread pudding drizzled with caramel sauce and served with a scoop of ice-cream.

I've been told "stressed" spelled backwards is "desserts" so it must mean we should eat desserts in time of stress. We were out to prove that point. We dug into the delicious treat and said little while we savored the wonderful flavors.

Dee Dee shook her empty spoon in my direction. "Trixie, I'm thankful you'll be staying with us. Maybe this Detective Sams will have all this sorted out in no time."

I hoped Dee Dee was right. "In the meantime, I have this article I'm working on that needs to be finished. If y'all don't mind I'd like to do more research on this Mr. Ghoston. He lived up on Lookout Mountain. I'd like to go back and interview the local historian."

Nana's eyes popped wide open. "Of course we don't mind." She wiped her mouth with her cloth napkin. "Let's go."

I should have known she'd be up for an adventure. I didn't know if taking on this research was in my best interest right now, but I had to get my mind on something other than seeing Annie's body in the freezer. I knew Harv would expect a report when I called him back tonight, and I wanted to be ready to share I was working on the story.

"Hey, I need to go to the ladies' room. Anybody want to come with me?" Dee Dee used to go to the bathroom at the drop of a hat. But since she'd been wearing *the patch,* her trips had been cut in half. It was nothing short of a miracle.

"I'll go with you," Nana said.

"Y'all go ahead while I call the lady I want to interview and see if she's available. We'll meet in the lobby when you're through." I placed a call to Tilly Andrews. She assured me she'd be home.

We took off in Dee Dee's rented car. And I mean *literally* took off. Dee drove like she was in a race on the Talladega Speedway, dodging in and out of cars at a speed leaving you dizzy. We almost clipped a Mercedes when she changed lanes. "Slow down, girl. We're not going to a fire."

"You're just a worry wart, Trix. I've been driving a long time. Who has all the speeding tickets from Vans Valley?" She guffawed at my expense.

Nana had to get in on the fun. "Yeah, Missy. Isn't that the kot calling the pettle black?" Her tongue twisted around the words of the common cliché. We burst into laughter. I glanced over to the car next to us. They stared at us like we'd grown extra heads. I told the girls, which triggered another bout of laughter. It was good to let go of the tension for a little while.

We drove through the little village of St. Elmo's at the bottom of Lookout Mountain. I took in the charming area of antique stores, restaurants, and ice cream shops.

"Stop!"

"Dee pull over! Something's wrong with Nana."

CHAPTER NINE

I turned around to discover the reason for Nana's outburst, my heart pounding like a jackhammer. Was it a heart attack?

"Nana, what's the matter? Do we need to take you to the emergency room?" She wasn't holding her chest. Good sign. What was that big smile doing on her face?

"Oh, I'm fine sweetie. I just saw the incline and wanted to take a ride. Wouldn't that be fun?"

"Nana, you are going to be the death of me yet." That is, if I didn't kill Nana first.

"Come on, Trixie. Let's grab life by the horns and make a spur-of-the-moment decision." Dee Dee pulled over to the side of the road and turned toward me. "It'll be fun."

I looked at the incline car and followed the tracks straight up to the top of the mountain. It didn't look like fun to me, but Dee Dee was right. Why not? "Okay, let's do it."

"I knew you'd break, Trixie." Dee Dee laughed with Nana like that was the funniest thing anyone had ever said.

Standing in the cold, waiting for the incline to arrive was not my idea of fun. I buttoned my coat and tightened my scarf. I withdrew the pamphlet from my pocket and read about the railway.

During the railroad boom of the 1880's, a luxury hotel resort was developed on the mountaintop that was serviced by a simple narrow gauge railway. However, in November of 1895, a new, broader gauge passenger railway simply known as "The Incline" opened to easily whisk residents and visitors up and down the steepest part of Lookout Mountain.

Built by John Crass and the Lookout Mountain Incline Railway Company, The Incline is a technical marvel that at its extreme, reaches an incline of 72.7%, making it one of the steepest passenger railways in the world. The original coal-burning steam engines were replaced by two 100-horse-power motors in 1911, but other than that the railway hasn't changed very much in its more than 100 years of operation.

By the time the ride was over, I couldn't wait to get my feet back on level ground.

"Admit it, Trixie, wasn't that fun?"

"About as much fun as having a gynecological exam."

"Well, it depends on how good looking the doctor is," Nana quipped.

"Nana!" Where Nana had the ability to make me blush or want to hide my head in the sand, Dee Dee was able to take her like a trooper.

"Oh, Nana. You're too funny." She drew her into a big bear hug encompassing most of Nana. "I love you."

Nana turned to me and smirked. "Well, I'm glad somebody loves me."

"Oh, Nana. I love you, too." It was my turn to give Nana a hug. "Come on ladies, we have to get up the mountain if we want to make it to my appointment on time."

Dee Dee zoomed around the curves as fast as she could without leaving the road. My stomach lurched as the butterflies tried to escape. I had a death grip on the door-handle and my knuckles had turned white by the time we arrived at the top of the mountain.

"What's the name of the street, Trix?" I wondered how Dee Dee could talk so calmly, but when I glanced her way she was as cool as a cucumber. "Isn't the snow beautiful? This is my kinda snow – when it sticks to the ground and not the roads."

When I gathered my wits, which were scattered all over the car, I looked at my note. "It's Mountain Way, Dee." The GPS lead us right to the door of Tilly Morrison, a long-time historian of Lookout Mountain and Chattanooga. She lived in a cute little cottage built to look like a log cabin.

I hoped three strange women – I mean strangers – standing on her doorstep didn't scare her. I failed to mention I'd have company with me. A little sprite of a lady opened the door. "Come in, come in out of the cold." She grabbed Nana's arm and practically dragged her inside.

"I assume one of you is Trixie Beaumont?" Her laughter filled the room. "I guess I should have found out for sure before I welcomed you into my house."

"Don't you worry one bit Tilly. If I may call you Tilly." Dee Dee stuck out her hand and Tilly reciprocated with a handshake. "I'm Dee Dee Lamont and this is Trixie." She pulled me up beside her. "And this is her great-aunt. We just call her Nana." Nana stepped up and offered her hand.

"Please, have a seat." The living area of Tilly's cottage contained furniture consistent with a log cabin theme. The sofa and chairs boasted rustic pine log frames. A fire crackled in the fireplace. The warmth and the glow of the fire made the room cozy and welcoming.

We removed our coats and made ourselves comfortable. I wasn't sure where to start. There were a lot of blanks to fill in on this case and I hoped Tilly would be able to fill in the missing pieces.

"Wait just a minute while I get the research material I've found." Tilly went into a study to retrieve what she needed, and returned with full arms. "This is a case I've been keeping up with over the years. It's not often we get a famous member of the Dixie Mafia living in our little community. I hope it will be the last – his murder left a dark shadow on our mountain." She spread the contents of her laden arms on a coffee table made of the same heavy wood as the rest of the set.

"That's what I'd call a passel of information," Nana said.

"You can say that again."

I could tell right off these two were going to be a lot of help. Then again, maybe not. I rolled my eyes automatically. Not a good idea.

"I saw that, Missy. I may be old, but I'm not stupid." It never failed Nana could pick up on my eye-rolls and would call me on it every time. If truth be told, I get impatient with Nana more often than not. I thought of all the adult children taking care of their parents and wondered how they kept their patience. I sent up a quick prayer for them and Mama. *Lord, please give these brave souls the patience and love they need to care for their parents. Help them remember the love their parents showered on them.*

"Sorry, Nana."

I turned and addressed Tilly to get the topic back on track. "Tilly, what can you tell us about Bobby Lee Ghoston?"

CHAPTER TEN

Bobby Lee grew up here on the mountain," Tilly said with confidence. I remember his parents – good people. He got into a little trouble as a teenager, but nothing serious. He hung around with another local youngster, Tad Hopkins. When those two got together it spelled t-r-o-u-b-l-e with a capital T."

"Were they ever arrested?" Since Dee Dee had helped with several of my articles, she felt comfortable asking questions. I didn't mind. She not only helped me with work, she helped me get my feet back on the ground when Wade's indiscretion knocked me flat on my back. Her strong faith during the sudden death of her husband was a never-ending example to me. My faith had grown under her care, but I strove to have the kind of faith Dee Dee possessed.

"Yes, they were, but I don't remember what it was for. Since they were teenagers at the time, I doubt you'd be able to find out. After they graduated from high school, they settled down. Both of them got married and they opened a furniture store together. Nobody was surprised when they became business partners."

"Where was their business located? It wasn't on the mountain was it?" I took notes and recorded the conversation for later reference.

"No, there's not much room on the mountain for businesses. It was located in Rossville outside of Chattanooga. Are you familiar with Highway 27 North?" I nodded. "It's located along that road."

Anyway, they seemed to be doing well. Both of them had nice, and

I do mean *nice* houses. Tad and his wife had one child, a daughter, and Bobby Lee didn't have any children." Tilly leaned forward and looked around the room as if someone else might hear our conversation. "You know what the sad thing is?"

We shook our heads.

"She was barely a teenager when her father died of a heart attack." Tilly hung her head. "It was a shame because her mama had run off with someone and left Tad to raise her. She didn't have a mama or a daddy."

Nana took her turn at questioning, "Oh my, what happened to her?"

"Ladies, before I continue, I've been a terrible hostess, how about some tea and homemade cookies?"

My tummy was quite full, but Dee Dee spoke up. "I'd love some cookies."

"Me, too, if it's not too much trouble," Nana chimed in.

I swanny I sometimes wondered if Nana had a tapeworm. That woman could eat more than Dee Dee and me together and she never gained an ounce. I hated to whine but, no fair.

Tilly gave me a questioning look. "Sounds lovely." She went to the kitchen to prepare our snack.

"We just ate y'all." I like to eat as much as the next person, but I needed to finish my interview.

"Lighten up, Trix. It's rude not to accept food when offered in someone's home." Dee Dee smiled to soften her words.

"You're right. What's a few hundred more calories?"

"Well, I know any calories that go through my lips are going to wind up on my hips, but I don't want to live life worried to death about being a little overweight." That statement was so Dee Dee. She strived to live life to the fullest and instead of wallowing in worry she looked at problems as challenges. What she couldn't handle she gave to the One who could. The one time I thought she wouldn't come out of the doldrums, was when she was accused of murder in Dahlonega, Georgia. I was so happy when Dee Dee was absolved of any involvement.

She hit the target more often than I did though. I tried, but I still enjoyed a good pity-party every now and then. I have to admit, since I'd reconnected with Dee Dee my ability to handle difficult situations had become easier and my faith had grown in the process. *Thank you God, for good friends.*

"Here ya' go!" Tilly interrupted my musings when she returned holding a tray laden with cookies and a teapot. I jumped up to help.

"Those cookies do look good, Tilly." Suddenly I was hungry again. She served everyone then resumed her story.

"Now where was I? Oh yeah, I was telling you about Tad's death that left his poor daughter without a caring parent."

"Do you remember her name?"

She gazed at the ceiling as if she'd find the answer written there. "Don't hold me to it, but I think it's Tabitha."

I wrote as Tilly continued.

"Well, Bobby Lee stepped up and took over as her guardian. He and his wife raised her just like they would their own. She never lacked for anything. I heard she was hard to handle for a while during her teens. I suppose those years aren't easy for any of us. Anyway, she went off to college until the unbelievable happened."

"What was that, Tilly?" Dee Dee and I asked in unison.

Bobby Lee's murder. It was terrible. They found him in one of his warehouses and I heard it was not a pretty sight. You've heard of people losing their heads. Well, he definitely lost his." A little shiver shook her body.

"And they never found out who committed the murder?" The sleuth inside me was intrigued.

"No they didn't, but the rumors flew. People were saying he was part of the Dixie Mafia, and they were cashing in on a payment."

I wondered if I'd gotten myself in deeper than was safe, and wondered what Beau would say about this new twist.

"What do you think, Tilly?"

"I guess anything is possible. One thing I know for sure is they lived high on the hog. The best of everything, nice house, new cars and that young'un had everything her heart desired. I've wondered from time to time if the furniture business was that lucrative." She shook her head in wonderment.

Dee Dee looked at her Minnie Mouse watch. Her clothes more likely than not, matched her personality – bold and colorful. Today she wore black pants with a bright red sweater covered in snowflakes. With the Christmas season arriving, she'd wear a holiday-themed outfit until the New Year arrived. I'd love to dress as bold, but I usually stuck to my brown, beiges, and pastel colors. I didn't like to draw attention to myself, but that was a lost cause with Dee Dee and Nana in tow.

She pointed to her timepiece. "We'd better be going if we want to get off the mountain before it gets dark. Do we need to go by the B&B to pick up your things?"

"No. I've got enough for tonight, I just need to check in and let Detective Sams know where I'll be staying. We can go by tomorrow and gather my luggage and car."

I hoped and prayed Nana hadn't ordered the Elves to tuck us in tonight. I didn't think I could handle them. "Thank you so much Tilly for taking the time to talk with us. You've been the perfect hostess. I'll be sure and let you know when the article's published, and I'll give you credit for your help."

She raised her hand. "It wasn't anything. I'm glad I could help." Tilly gathered the material spread out on her coffee table and returned it to a box. "Here, Trixie, you can take this with you and go through it at your leisure."

I took a few pictures of Tilly and we said our good-byes. We were going out the door when Nana's foot slipped on a patch of ice. She straightened her arms to cushion her fall. I heard a sickening crack when she hit the ground. A shrill scream pierced the evening air.

CHAPTER ELEVEN

"Mama, don't worry, she's all right."

Nana yelled from the hospital bed. "I'm okay, Betty Jo. You should see my hot pink cast."

"Oh, dear! Tell me what happened. Do I need to come to Chattanooga?"

"No, Mama, you don't need to come. Nana just slipped on a patch of ice. Dee Dee and I have this under control. They're getting Nana's discharge papers ready and we'll be able to leave. We're going back to the hotel as soon as we leave here. Mama, I've got more bad news." There followed a big sigh on the other end of the phone.

"Go ahead. I can handle anything but another dead body."

An involuntary gasp escaped my lips.

"You found another one didn't you? Trixie, what am I going to do with you? Every time you go on an assignment a dead body turns up."

She was right. My greatest nightmare of becoming Jessica Fletcher was coming true. I always said I wouldn't want to be her friend because bodies turned up everywhere she went. Now the same thing was happening to me.

"Annie, our teacher, turned up in the deep freeze. We've already been questioned so I don't see any problems arising from the incident. Of course, we won't have any classes and the detective wants me to stick around a few days, but I have an article I can work on while I'm here. It'll be okay, Mama."

"Please keep me up to date on what's happening and ask Nana to call me when she feels like it. By the way, Jill called and said you didn't answer your phone. She was concerned about you."

Jill, my daughter, attends the University of Georgia. "I had my phone turned off during the interview with Tilly. If she calls back please don't tell her about my discovery. I don't want her to worry while she's at school."

"How's Nana doing?"

I scooted back into the screened-in area where Nana was flirting with a handsome young doctor. "She's doing fine, Mama."

We talked a few more minutes before saying goodbye. Dee Dee arrived from a trip to the gift shop. I didn't see the snacks she left to buy, but I figured she'd stashed them in her behemoth purse. She had a habit of carrying a bag the size of a small overnight case. Today was no different. She patted the colorful bag by her side.

"Let me know when you need a little pick-me-up. I couldn't decide what to buy, so I got one of everything." She laughed and I couldn't help but smile. Just being around Dee Dee lifted my spirits.

"How's the patient?" Dee Dee pulled out a bear with its arm in a sling. "I found this for Nana."

"Oh how cute. Nana will love it. She's doing fine – look for yourself." We entered the enclosed area. Nana held out her arm while a male nurse signed her cast. She flashed him a big smile.

"Oh, there you are Dee Dee. Come look at my cast. Isn't it the coolest color?" Nana stuck out her arm so Dee Dee could get a good look. The hospital smell suddenly triggered memories of my knee replacement surgery. I was devastated when I realized I couldn't put the procedure off any longer. My years of participating in sports and my fall precipitated the surgery at such a young age. All recipients of knee replacements have to attend a class to learn about the operation – I was the youngest in attendance.

"Trixie!" Nana's voice brought me back to reality. "Want to sign my cast?"

"Sure." She handed me a Sharpie the nurses had provided. Nana's doctor came in and explained her care. Keeping her arm elevated was going to be a challenge. She possessed more energy than Dee Dee and me together. I eyed her laughing and joking with the nurses, but I wondered how she'd feel after the pain medicine wore off.

"She's eating up the attention isn't she?" Dee Dee pulled out a pack of peanut butter crackers and offered them to me.

"Yep, she's a ham for sure. I'm just concerned when the drugs wear off she's going to be in for a rude awakening." I grasped the offered snack and quickly ate one of the crackers.

"Yeah, we need to keep her on a four hour schedule so that won't happen. I guess we'd better get her back to the hotel and elevate that arm. The doc says it'll keep the swelling down." She grabbed the crackers from my hand and stuffed one in her mouth.

"Hey, get your own. Don't you have something else you can eat in that suitcase of yours?"

She rummaged around and brought out a package of pretzels. "Here, you can have these. And don't make fun of my purse. How many times have I come to the rescue when you needed something?"

I feigned contrition. "Touché. Sorry for making fun of it." My phone rang, jarring my nerves. Dee Dee said she'd get Nana ready to go while I talked on the phone. I didn't recognize the number.

"Hello."

"Ms. Beaumont? Trixie?" The familiar voice came through loud and clear.

"Hello, Detective Sams. Is there something I can do for you?" My stomach churned like an old timey washing machine.

"Yes, I need to talk with you tonight. Some things have turned up changing the direction of this case quite a bit. Could you come down to the precinct now?"

I told her about Nana's fall. "Let me take her back to the hotel first." Once again, I was glad Dee Dee had tagged along to help with Nana. Lord knows I needed all the help I could get. I offered a quick prayer. *Thank you, God, for good friends.*

CHAPTER TWELVE

I left Nana in Dee Dee's care while I went to see what Detective Sams wanted. During the drive downtown my thoughts swirled like the leaves in a whirlwind. Being unfamiliar with the streets, I circled around twice before I turned on the right road. The station was located at the bottom of The Bluff, so it didn't take but a few minutes to arrive.

The station was small with sparse furnishings. I assumed it was a satellite to a bigger facility. A young lady in uniform sat behind a battered desk talking on a two-way radio giving instructions to someone on the other end. She offered me a genuine smile.

"Hi, I'm Trixie Beaumont, and I'm here to see Detective Sams," I said when she was finished.

A look of sympathy quickly replaced her smile.

"Detective Sams is expecting you." She jumped up from her chair and opened the office door, stuck her head in and announced my arrival. The detective indicated for me to enter. My heart rate quickened as I entered her sanctuary.

"What did you call me in for, Detective?" I noticed Sergeant Gary Sargent sitting in front of a desk that took up most of the room.

"I'm afraid it's not good news." Detective Sams pointed toward a chair. "Would you take a seat please?"

Grateful for the offer, I sat down before I fell down. The air crackled with tension while I waited for her to tell me the fateful news.

"Please tell me why I'm here."

"Annie's death is officially a murder."

Duh, that was a no-brainer. She didn't jump into the freezer herself.

She placed her arms on the desk-top and leaned in. "We know Annie was poisoned and we know it was in her tea, we just haven't narrowed it down to the particular poison. But that will come out in due time."

"Why are you telling me all of this?"

"It seems she had a liking for a very unusual tea. One she special ordered." The detective gave another pregnant pause. Why in the world couldn't she talk faster? My bottled blonde hair was going to turn gray if she didn't wrap this up.

"What does any of this have to do with me?"

"Trixie, we found a bag of Rose Petal Green Tea in your room. They're running tests on it now. We also found your fingerprints on her teacup and teapot."

"But we had tea together, and I was helping her serve. Of course my prints were on the teacup." Oh – my – goodness, my breaths came erratically. The room began to spin, and the detective's voice sounded far away.

"Put your head between your legs." It wasn't an easy feat to accomplish, but I managed. My breathing slowed and the room stopped spinning. I righted myself and braced for the rest of Detective Sam's speech.

"I'm sorry to be the bearer of bad news, but it doesn't look good for you. It's important that you not leave the area until we give you the go ahead."

"I don't understand. I didn't have any reason to kill Annie."

"That's one thing we haven't figured out yet," Sergeant Gary Sargent said. "But we're working on it." He actually had the audacity to smile. Maybe it was payback for me laughing at his name. He seemed to be enjoying my discomfort way too much.

What was I going to do? Would I have to find the killer myself? My mind flashed back to the conversation I'd had with Dee Dee earlier. I knew she'd do anything she could to help.

"Trixie," Detective Sams stared at me with a look of concern, "are you all right? I was talking to you, but you didn't seem to be hearing me."

"I'm sorry. This has been a shock to me."

"As a person of interest I'll be questioning you again, soon." The detective shuffled through a file. "Let's see, you're staying at the Chattanooga Choo-Choo?"

"Yes ma'am."

"Be sure and let us know if you decide to stay somewhere else."

I nodded my head and hoped the end of this conversation was near. I didn't believe the discussion could get any worse. It did. Detective Sams wasn't through with me yet.

"Oh, one more thing. Your reputation precedes you. I'm aware of your amateur sleuthing skills. However, I do not want you to even think about getting involved like that with this case. I assure you my department will do everything in our power to treat you fairly. If you're not guilty, then you shouldn't have anything to worry about."

Easy for you to say when it's not your freedom on the line.

"That's all for tonight. You are free to go."

I left the station wondering what hit me. I didn't see that one coming. I knew I'd discovered the body, but I had no reason to be worried about being a person of interest or more plainly put – a suspect. How and why did the tea end up in my room? The word *framed* popped into my mind.

That had to be it. I'd been framed. The question was "why"? I yawned several times driving back to the hotel. The stress of the past couple of days hit me full-force making it hard to keep my eyes open.

I stealthily opened the door to the sound of Nana's snores. I wondered if Dee Dee was asleep, when her head popped up from her pillow. She stage whispered. "Hey, girl. I waited up to see what the detective wanted. By the look on your face it wasn't good."

I took off my outerwear, slipped off my boots and tip-toed to Dee Dee's bed. She scooted over and I sat beside her. She gave my arm a hearty squeeze. "Come on. Spit it out, girl. What did she say that made you look like you'd just lost your favorite camera?"

"Annie's death is officially considered a murder and I'm a person of interest." A lone tear slid down my cheek.

"Oh, no. How in the world did they come up with that theory? I know you found the body, but surely they aren't basing their beliefs on that alone."

"Sams said during the sweep of my room they discovered a bag of the specially ordered tea that Annie drinks. And it didn't help my fingerprints were on her tea cup and the tea kettle."

Dee Dee shook her head. "How did the tea get in your room? It almost sounds like someone was trying to set you up."

I sat up a little straighter. "I thought the same thing, Dee. I think somebody tried to frame me, but I don't know why."

A loud snort startled me, and I gave Dee Dee a questioning look. I feared we'd woken up Nana, but she turned over and the snoring pattern started again.

"We'd better try to get some sleep. I don't think we can figure this out tonight." My thoughts were jumbled as a batch of scrambled eggs. I'd have to wait until tomorrow to call Harv and Beau.

"Okay, we can talk about it in the morning when our brains are fresh." Dee Dee reached over and gave me a quick hug.

Unfortunately, I was afraid morning wasn't going to look much better.

CHAPTER THIRTEEN

Morning arrived as gray as my mood. I looked over to discover Dee Dee smiling at me. She held a book titled "Cowgirls Don't Cry." Nana was still asleep, and I supposed the pain medicine they'd given her at the hospital kept her from waking at her usual dawn-thirty.

"Hey, Trix. How ya' feeling this morning?" Dee Dee's greeting reminded me of summer birds chirping as the sun came up.

"Not much better than last night. I feel like I dreamed all night. But the real nightmare is now that I'm wide awake. What am I going to do?" What in the world was I going to tell Mama and Beau? Poor Beau, he was going to wish he'd never married me. Who wanted to be married to someone who discovered dead bodies for a past-time?

Nana stirred and emitted a little moan. Bless her heart; she didn't need a broken arm. Her eyes flew open. "Oh my goodness! What time is it? I must have overslept, the sun is shining so bright."

"Nana, you need your rest to heal. Don't worry about over sleeping. Remember, we're on vacation and we can lie in bed all day if we want." Dee Dee had such a calming effect on Nana.

"I guess you're right. Oh, my arm is aching. It hurts more than it did last night."

I gave Dee Dee a knowing look. I figured the pain would catch up with her. She's not as young as she thinks she is. I caught a glimpse of the hot pink cast and smiled. I had to admit Nana had a way of making the most of life. Though she'd stepped on my last nerve more than once, I was proud of the way she took life by the horns and lived like there was no tomorrow. She had never been one to be preachy about her faith, but the fact that she got up every morning, depending on God to be her companion during the day, had been an example I yearned to follow.

"I'm sorry Nana, do you need more pain medicine?" Before she could answer, Dee Dee jumped up and retrieved a glass of water and the medicine bottle.

"Here ya' go, Nana." She handed her a pill large enough for a horse and waited on her to take it.

"Thanks, Dee. Says right here on the bottle not to take on an empty stomach. Guess we'd better hurry and get Nana some breakfast."

We spent the next thirty minutes getting dressed and helping Nana get ready. She insisted on wearing a hot pink outfit to match her cast. We headed downtown in my P.T. Cruiser to scope out a good place to eat. We settled on McDonalds.

I opted for an egg biscuit, Dee Dee decided on an Egg McMuffin, and Nana chose a pancake breakfast. Coffee was the drink of choice. We chose a table by a window. Even though it was cold outside, the sun had burned off the fog. Sitting inside someone could easily mistake it for a spring day. No ice from the night before remained. I was thankful for that. We didn't need Nana falling again – or me either.

As I looked out the window I felt like an elephant sat on my chest. Despair cloaked me like a winter shawl.

"Trixie, do you want to talk about it?"

I looked at Dee Dee, then at Nana. Did I want to involve Nana in the latest turn of events? I figured there was no way around it since she was staying with us. I needed to talk to Dee Dee about helping me and it would be a moot point trying to leave Nana out of the loop.

"Talk about what?" Nana asked.

Dee Dee nodded her head. "Last night Detective Sams named Trixie a person of interest in Annie's death." She went on to tell her more about the tea and circumstantial evidence against me. I was glad she could tell her. I fiddled with my biscuit, listening to my life described like the six o'clock news. I prayed I wouldn't cry in front of Nana. I didn't want to worry her. *Lord give me strength.*

Her posture stiffened. "What? Why would they do that?" I thought I saw smoke coming from Nana's ears when she realized the gravity of the situation.

Dee Dee reached over and patted Nana's hand. "Don't worry Nana. I'll make sure Trixie's found innocent. No way will I let Trixie take the rap for something she didn't do."

"Worried? I'm not worried. She didn't do anything, and she has nothing to hide! I don't see any reason why we can't solve this case just like the others. Tell me what you need me to do." Nana held up her injured arm. "Just because I have a cast doesn't mean I can't help."

That's what I was afraid of. Yes, Nana helped solve a couple of crimes, but she was kidnapped when we got a little too close to the culprits on Tybee Island and I didn't want that to ever happen again.

"Well, Trixie, what do you say. Should we make out a suspect list? Surely the murderer had to be someone staying at the bed and breakfast," Dee Dee said.

"That would be the logical place to start."

After we cleaned up our table, we decided to go back to the hotel and make a list. The pain medicine Nana had taken kicked in by the time we arrived back at the Chattanooga Choo-Choo and she opted for a nap while Dee Dee and I worked in the lobby. I knew she must be tired if she was going to miss out on anything concerning Annie's murder.

CHAPTER FOURTEEN

We scoped out a corner in the expansive lobby where we'd be out of the way and out of earshot. Off-white wingback chairs stitched with delicate red flowers sat on a red and beige area rug. The sun shone through an abundance of windows, filling the atrium with shards of sunlight. A couple holding hands were at the counter, making goo-goo eyes at each other. I assumed they had reservations for the honeymoon suite. My cheeks heated at the memory of mine and Beau's honeymoon.

I waited for Dee Dee to visit the ladies room. I picked up a brochure boasting the history of the hotel.

> *The Terminal Station was erected in 1908, with its centerpiece – a magnificent dome – that rose majestically over the concourse. Built of steel and concrete and buttressed by huge brick arches, the dome rested on four steel supports 75 feet apart. Suspended from the ceiling were four brass chandeliers, each with 40 lights circling an 18-inch opal globe. From an architectural standpoint, this dome over the entire 68 x 82 foot general waiting rooms was the most attractive design feature of its time.*
>
> *It was on the underside of this dome, the part in view above the waiting room, that the only attempt to decorate in colors was made – artistic plaster embellishments of*

heraldic emblems, which are now fully restored. The dome was truly lavish and beautiful in its different prismatic colors, especially when lighted at night.

I looked up and studied the splendor of the paintings.

"What 'cha doing?" Dee Dee came back and followed my gaze.

"I've been reading about the history of the hotel. Isn't the dome beautiful? I read where John Staten of Boston opened Stanton House in 1870. It was ahead of its time with the placement of a recently invented telephone in the lobby. And it had electric lights."

Dee Dee laughed and sat down in a chair next to mine. "You sound like a history lesson."

"Since I've been working for the magazine it's in my blood. Anyway, let me finish. By the end of the century it wasn't doing so well, so Stanton sold it to the Southern Railroad in 1905 and they leveled the old hotel in 1906 to make way for the railroad station."

She craned her neck to take in the entire ceiling. "It really is beautiful. Now," Dee Dee pulled out a tablet from her gigantean bag, "let's get down to working on this list. We don't have a minute to waste."

"You've got that right. And I'm supposed to be working on the Ghoston murder for Harv. I don't know how I'm going to finish it before the deadline he gave me." I separated the branches of the fern and looked out into the lobby. I had a great view. "I feel sorry for Tilly. She was beside herself over Nana's fall."

Dee Dee guffawed.

"What's so funny?"

"I'm sorry Trixie," Dee Dee snorted. "I had this picture in my mind of Tilly standing beside herself."

I smiled. "Well, put that way I could see how you'd think it was funny. Unfortunately, I'm not in a funny mood right now."

"I understand. I was just trying to lighten the mood. We have to laugh some, Trix, or we'll end up crying and that won't do anybody good." She reached in her bag and quickly retrieved a pen. I was in awe. "Tell me who all the other participants in the workshop were and a little bit about them. We'll have to find out where they're staying. Got any ideas how to get that information?"

"Detective Sams?"

"See, you made a funny. Good for you." She wrote something on the paper and underlined it with a flourish. "Now, tell me a name."

I lifted my head and stared into space trying to remember my classmates. Bodene's name popped in my head first. "Okay, Bodene Tate."

Dee Dee looked at me with raised eyebrows. "Sounds like a good Southern name."

"Yeah, I hope he doesn't represent all Southerners because he'd give us a bad name. He's this big, burly guy and he's all tatted up."

"That doesn't sound too bad," Dee Dee said.

"No, but it's what he said that got everyone's attention. He told the class that he'd been in prison and he wanted to write his memoir of prison life. According to him, "he didn't kill nobody," and he wants to write a book to clear his name. He said he didn't have any writing experience, but he thought it would be pretty easy."

"Wow, he sounds like a character. Were all your classmates of this caliber?" A giggle escaped Dee Dee's lips.

"No, it was a very eclectic group. There was Lori Wilson, not only is she cover-model beautiful, she's smart, too. She's the editor of an ad driven magazine, *The Tennessean*. She has aspirations of being an editor for a women's magazine, and with her ambition and gorgeous presence, I believe she just might."

"Doesn't sound like much of a killer." Dee Dee shook a cramp from her hand.

"You and I've both learned you can't go by what someone looks like to finger them as a killer."

"Yeah, we learned the hard way didn't we?"

"There's something about her though that raised my hackles. Annie asked if they had ever met and Lori told her "no." But the look Lori gave Annie could have melted butter. I think there must be some bad blood between them. Why else would she look at her like that?"

"I don't know, but I'm going to put a star by her name."

"I think she mentioned living in Chattanooga. She might be a good suspect to start with." I separated the leaves of the fern for another check and staring back at me was a pair of dark, beady eyes. I yelped, jumping from my chair.

CHAPTER FIFTEEN

Dee Dee followed suit, and sent pad and pen flying. "What in the tarnation's going on, Trix. Why'd you do that?"

"Somebody was spying on us." I grabbed the arm of a uniformed staff member for an explanation. The older woman's head seemed crooked, and then I realized it was because her hair was leaning sideways. I hoped it was a wig. She reached up to straighten it, now it leaned the other way. "Why were you watching us? You could get in trouble for that."

A Cheshire Cat grin spread across her face. "Yeah, well everyone around here is a little jumpy and I heard you mention poisoning someone." She tugged at my hand. "Let me go. I should tell my supervisor about this. Come to think of it, I might just bypass my supervisor and go straight to the police."

"Go ahead, we don't have anything to hide." I let go of her sleeve and gulped, that wasn't exactly true. I suspected it wouldn't bode well for me with Detective Sams if she discovered what we'd been discussing. Too late to worry about that now. "Wait!"

She scurried off like a squirrel chased by a dog. Dee Dee stood totem pole still with her mouth agape.

"My goodness," I turned toward Dee Dee, "what do you think she really heard?" I sat back down before my legs gave out.

Dee Dee found her voice. "I don't know, but there's nothing we can do about it now. Let's get back to our list." With her bottom turned heavenward she retrieved her pen and tablet. She sat, scooted around for comfort, and placed the tablet on her lap with aplomb. "Shoot."

I stuck my finger and thumb out and pulled an imaginary trigger. "Bang."

"Funny, Trix. Very funny." She tried to keep a straight face, but failed miserably. Her laughter echoed in the large, open lobby. "Thanks for the comic relief. We needed that. Just hope nobody was spying on us."

"That's for sure. All right, who do we have on the list so far?" My shoulders relaxed a bit and my breathing settled to almost normal. I had a feeling it would be short-lived.

"We have Bodene Tate and Lori Wilson," Dee Dee said.

"There's Tippi 'with-an-i' Colston." I gave Dee Dee the queen's wave. Tippi's a gorgeous redhead. The problem is she knows it and she holds her nose just a little higher than most. I tried being friendly with her, but she didn't warm up any." I recalled something about her I'd forgotten until now. "Hey, I just remembered she was outside Annie's door when I was in the hallway. I need to tell Detective Sams about this."

"Yeah, that might take the investigation in another direction – away from you. Why don't you call her now?" Dee Dee reached in her bag and pulled out her phone. It always amazed me how fast she could find something in her mammoth bags. "Here, you can use mine."

I rummaged around in my purse for the detective's business card. I finally located it on the bottom. I handed it to Dee Dee. "Can you read the number; I don't have my reading glasses on?"

Dee Dee reached for the glasses she'd pushed up on her head and pulled them down into place. "Here ya go – 555-4582."

I punched in the numbers and put it on speaker phone so Dee Dee could hear. After two rings a woman answered. After I asked for Detective Sams, she informed me that the detective was away on business and asked if I wanted to leave a message. I'd be sitting on pins and needles until she called back.

I handed Dee Dee her phone. "Write down George Buchanan as well." It was painful to remember the scene where Annie berated him. "I believe if I was George I'd want to kill her."

"Why?" Dee Dee asked with raised eyebrows.

"It was terrible Dee. Annie had asked each of us to write a paper. She read them out loud and then critiqued them. After she read George's paper she said "this is an example of how not to write" and then shredded it. Everyone just sat there in shock. Poor ole' George didn't take it so well. He threw back his chair, threatened Annie, then fled the room."

"Sounds like another candidate for a person of interest. I swanny, I don't know why the detective focused on you. I'm putting a star by his name, too."

Dee Dee tapped her pencil on her tablet. "Getting back to George. When you tell Detective Sams about Tippi, you need to tell her about George, too. Who else do we need to write down?"

"Amanda Holbrook. She reminds me of myself when Wade divorced me. Instead of a chip, she has a boulder on her shoulder." Dee Dee grinned at my rhyme. "She's been put in a position where she has to find a job to support herself and her children. She wrote for pleasure, now she wants to write professionally. Sounds a lot like me, doesn't it."

"That may have been you when you first moved back to Vans Valley, but it isn't you now. You've grown so much Trixie. I'm real proud of you." She rewarded me with a wide smile.

"Thanks Dee. I couldn't have done it without your help and support." I reached over and squeezed her hand. I had no doubt Dee Dee would be there for the long haul.

"Anyway, Amanda definitely harbors a lot of anger, but it seems to be directed at her ex-husband. I don't see any reason she'd take it out on Annie."

"Yeah, but she was in the bed and breakfast so we need to write her down." Dee Dee wrote her name with a flourish.

"The only other person I can think of is Ladonna, the housekeeper. She was in the room when Annie told us she was feeling sick. I wonder if she's staying at the bed and breakfast? If so, it'd be easy to find her."

"Looks like we have us a bonafide suspect list. So far we have Bodene, Lori, Tippi, George, Amanda and Ladonna. Wow, that's six people."

I looked over Dee Dee's shoulder to see none other than Detective Sams and Sergeant Gary Sargent heading our way. "Quick, hide the list. Here comes the detective."

CHAPTER SIXTEEN

Quick thinking Dee Dee opted for a foolproof method of hiding the names. She shoved the tablet under her ample bottom, and donned a smile, as innocent as a baby.

"Trixie." Detective Sams greeted me then she shot a questioning look toward Dee Dee.

"Hello, Detective. This is my good friend, Dee Dee Lamont."

Dee Dee stared at her mirror image. "Hi."

Detective Sams gave an approving look at Dee's outfit. Today she wore red slacks, a white top with a red and green sweater, in keeping with the holiday season. "Nice ensemble, Dee Dee."

"Why thank you," Dee Dee said, grinning ear to ear.

"Unfortunately, I'm not here to talk about clothes. I hear you ladies were making a hit list?"

What in the world? I guess that busybody reported us. Just when I thought things couldn't get worse – they did. I looked up to see Nana staggering toward us. I reached over and nudged Dee Dee and pointed toward Nana. We jumped up at the same time knocking into each other. Dee Dee, being a patron of the Woman's Department, won the round and I ended up back in my chair. She moved faster than I ever imagined she could. I hurried to catch up. With Dee Dee on one side and me on the other we guided Nana over to the chairs and sat her down. All the while Detective Sams and Sergeant Gary Sargent took in the scene wide-eyed.

Everybody gathered around and I sat in the chair opposite Nana. "What's the matter? Don't you feel good, Nana?"

She looked up and smiled. "Actually, I feel pretty good." She held up her hot pink cast. "See, no pain."

Dee Dee gasped. "Nana, did you take more of your pain medicine?"

"I just took two more," she shook her head, "I think it was just two." I wasn't feeling any better, so I thought I'd take a couple more. Now I don't feel a bit of pain. A little woozy though."

I lifted my head toward heaven. *Lord, give me strength and patience. Hurry please.* "Sorry about that, Detective. This is my great-aunt, Nana. As you can see she fell last night and broke her arm."

"I'm sorry to hear about that, ma'am. Now back to that list."

Nana piped up. "Are you here to question Trixie?" She slurred her words making it sound more like "Are you here to quesion Trixie?"

"Ma'am this is police business," Detective Sams said. "Someone needs to get this woman coffee. Or escort her back to bed."

"I'll be quiet." Nana dropped back against the cushion, cradling her cast in her good hand, her head swaying a bit from side to side.

The sergeant had his notepad out, ready to take down whatever I said.

"What list are you talking about?" I saw the tablet sticking out from under Nana. I held my breath hoping she wouldn't notice. No such luck.

Nana pulled it out and raised it high in the air. "What's this?"

CHAPTER SEVENTEEN

Four hands grabbed for the notebook. Detective Sams won, snatching it faster than a coon dog treeing a squirrel. "Let me see what we have here. Suspect list?"

"Uh, we were just brainstorming, Detective. It doesn't mean we were going to do anything with it. By the way, I wanted to tell you about Tippi Colston. She was right outside Annie's door when I went to visit her. And Annie tore up a paper George wrote. He threatened her before the whole class. You can ask them."

"I fully intend to. I don't think you'll need this list, so I'll just take it with me." She skimmed the list. "You've been busy, haven't you?" She ripped out the page Dee Dee made her notes on. "I told you before, I'd investigate this case to the fullest. When there is as much evidence as there is against you then you automatically shoot to the top of the list. It doesn't mean we won't look at others, but you need to leave it to the professionals."

Nana spoke up. "She is a professional. She's solved three cases already. And I helped."

"Yes ma'am, I'm sure she was an asset to those cases, but she's a person of interest in this one. That means hands-off. Do you understand?" Detective Sams looked from me to Dee Dee and back to me.

"I definitely understand what you said, Detective." I understood what she said, but it didn't mean I was going to keep my hands off this case. It was my bootie that was at risk of being thrown in the caboose, and I didn't trust the detective to clear my name.

"All right then, I'll be on my way. I don't want anyone else calling in with information you're sleuthing on your own."

Well my goodness, we were in agreement, I didn't want anyone calling in either.

"Let me know if you change hotels and I'll be in touch with you soon." She touched the bill of her hat with her hand, turned on her heel and sauntered out of the lobby. Sergeant Sargent gave me one last smirk before he hurried to catch up with the detective.

I looked over at Nana to find her sound asleep in the chair. Her mouth stood wide open and a little bit of drool slid down her lip. She snored like a bear.

Dee Dee's stomach emitted a growl louder than Nana's snoring. "Yikes, look at the time. No wonder I'm hungry. It's afternoon already." She glanced at Nana. "What are we going to do with her?"

"I'd like to get some lunch, but we need to wake her and take her back to the room first." I'd no sooner got the word "lunch" out of my mouth when her head popped up like a jack-in-the-box.

"Did someone mention food?" She shot us a glance. "I'm so hungry I could eat an elephant." I've seen Nana eat and she wasn't far off.

"Sounds good to me. Let's make a new list while we eat." I didn't want to waste a minute – even though she seemed sincere, Detective Sams most likely had more than one case on her hands. She needed the help, right?

A commotion in the lobby startled me from my musings, and I followed the sound. A couple of skipping elves led a rowdy group of children. I guess elves were big this time of year in Chattanooga.

"How about the Garden Restaurant for lunch?" Dee Dee offered. "It's located right off the lobby and Nana won't have far to walk."

"Sounds great, let's go." Nana jumped up, but sat right back down. "Whoa, not feeling as spry as I thought." Dee Dee laughed. I didn't think it was quite so funny. I needed to call Mama and see if she'd help with Nana, but I didn't want to interrupt her vacation. After lunch I had to make some calls.

I jumped when Alan Jackson's Chattahoochee rang out from my

purse. I forgot I'd changed the ring tone. I looked at the caller I.D. and groaned. "Hello, Harv."

"Trixie. You said you'd call me back. I waited as long as I could. We're on a deadline you know." I nodded in agreement, but Harv kept right on going. "Are you making any progress on the Ghoston murder?"

"Uh, I've been working on it Harv."

I waved for Dee Dee and Nana to go on to the restaurant without me. "I'll catch up. It's Harv." Dee Dee nodded and put her arm around Nana's waist as she led her forward.

"What's going on, Trixie?" Harv growled.

"I was just telling the girls to go eat without me, I'd catch up." Harv's a taskmaster for sure, but even he wouldn't object to me taking time to eat. "Harv, there's been a little hitch in my plans."

"A little hitch, Trixie? I don't like the sound of that." I heard Harv's squeaky desk chair. He needed to oil that old thing. I imagined him removing his feet from his desk and leaning over in a serious pose. "Spit it out, girl. I don't have all day."

I held back the tears, I didn't want to leave an impression I couldn't handle my job. "I found a dead body in the deep freeze," I sniffed.

"I thought I heard you say you found a body in the freezer. I know you didn't say that. Did you, Trixie?" It was time to put on my big girl panties and come clean with the truth.

"That's what I said." I gulped back a sob. "Now I'm a person of interest in the case."

"Who was it and how did you wind up in the middle of a murder investigation?"

"It was, Annie Henderson, my teacher, from the intensive workshop. I was the last person to be alone with her. When the police found poisoned tea in my room my fate was sealed. I'm their prime suspect. I was framed, Harv."

A crunch resonated through the phone. I supposed he'd bit down on his Tootsie Pop upon hearing the news. There was a prolonged silence before anyone spoke.

"Harv? Are you there?"

"Yes I'm here. I'm trying to think. I know this is a terrible situation, but you're strong and you can take this and turn it around to your advantage. I know you didn't kill that woman. Take this opportunity to write about being wrongly accused."

I pulled a tissue from my purse and blew my nose. "Uh, I guess I could do that." Maybe writing about the experience would keep my mind focused.

"Great, that settles it. I know you'll pull through this, Trixie. I have faith in you. Well, gotta go. Check in with me later." I heard a click indicating the conversation was over. I replaced the phone in my bag.

CHAPTER EIGHTEEN

I hurried to catch Dee Dee and Nana as fast as my knee allowed. They were studying their menus. "Did you order a sweet tea for me?"

"Does a dog like bones?" Dee Dee offered me a big grin.

"I'm taking that for a yes." I needed all the sugar I could get.

Nana reached over and patted my hand. "What's the matter sweetie, you look like you've lost your last friend."

"I just got through talking to Harv. It was all I could do to hold back the tears. He wants me to write an article about sleuthing out the real killer. He thinks my being a person of interest would help me write about being wrongly accused."

"Don't you worry that pretty little head of yours. Dee Dee and I will help (she drew out help into two syllables). Hay-ulp made me feel a tad better, and I grabbed the menu and quickly looked at the offerings as the waitress appeared. "I'll take the soup and sandwich combo." Dee Dee and Nana opted for the chicken salad on lettuce. We sat back to wait on our food.

I glanced at Nana and noticed her half-closed eyelids. A huge smile indicated her pain level had dropped. I'd have to keep a closer watch on her so she didn't overdose on her pain medicine. I'd ask Dee Dee later what she thought about asking Mama to come and help.

I nudged her and pointed toward Nana. "Looks like she's about to flake out on us."

"I heard that," Nana said. "I might be half asleep, but I'm not deaf. Anyway, I'm just looking at the back of my eyelids." Laughter floated around the table.

The waitress, laden down with food, approached our table. "Here ya' go." She served our delicious looking meal. "My name is Lisa. I hope you enjoy your food and let me know if you need anything." She sashayed across the room. Oh to be so young.

When our appetites were satisfied, Dee Dee sat back and wiped her mouth. She voiced my thoughts. "Trix, what are we going to do now that Detective Sams took our list?"

"Make another one. It shouldn't take long." Dee Dee retrieved her tablet and pen. In a matter of minutes we had a new list.

At times, a groggy Nana would revive and make a comment. We debated who we should visit first and decided on Lori Wilson. I remembered she lived in Chattanooga or close by.

"When we get back to the room I'll look up her name on my laptop." We finished our meal by ordering strawberry shortcake. We helped Nana back to our room and settled her in bed before heading out to interview Lori. I discovered she lived in Hixon right outside of Chattanooga.

It took us about twenty minutes to find her home. Thank goodness for a GPS. As Nana would say, "one of the greatest inventions since sliced bread." It was a pretty little area. Her house was a modest ranch style home reminiscent of the 60's and 70's architecture and located on lakefront property.

The same pretty face I remembered opened the door. "Hello, Trixie, come on in." She led us into a living room filled with antique furniture. Dee Dee's eyes bugged out.

"Wow, this is a treasure trove, Lori." I thought I saw Dee Dee lick her lips. Being the owner of an antiques store, the wheels of her collector's brain were hard at work. "Sarah, my assistant at the store, would have a heyday in here." She explained to Lori about her shop, Antiques Galore.

It was time to get down to business. "Lori, how well did you know Annie?" I noticed a fleeting expression of fear and then it was gone.

"Uh, why do you want to know?"

There was no reason to beat around the bush so I opted for the direct approach. "I don't know if you've heard, but I'm a person of interest in her murder. That really means I'm a suspect and according to Detective Sams, I'm the main suspect." Her eyes popped open and her mouth formed an O. There was no mistaking a moment of fear.

"What are you doing here?"

"We need your help if we're going to clear Trixie's name," Dee Dee said.

Lori fumbled around, found a remote control and turned off the television. "I don't know how I can help. I really didn't know Annie that well." She averted her eyes when she said she didn't know her. I didn't believe her.

"I remember her saying you looked familiar. I thought you might have met her and just didn't remember."

Faster than a chameleon changing colors, she transformed from a composed young lady to a ranting female.

"Look, you want the truth?"

Even though I wasn't so sure anymore, I nodded my head.

"I'll give you the truth. I don't care if that old bat is dead. She was my brother's teacher in college. Leonard was about to graduate when she failed him in English. He didn't have enough credits to walk with his class. He'd already invited his family and friends to the celebration. She was some wannabe writer who just couldn't cut it in the real world. So she took it out on her students."

Tears rolled down her bronze cheeks. "He was devastated. Not graduating with his class was the last straw and he started drinking again. He had a problem when he was a teenager, but he'd gotten back on track and was trying to get his degree. He had to study harder than most just to keep his head above water. Annie Hamilton," she spewed her name like venom, "wouldn't give him a break. Is that enough truth for you?" Her voice faded as if she was out of breath.

I looked over at wide-eyed Dee Dee. "Why couldn't he just walk, and then take the class in summer school, they do that all..."

"Because she accused him of cheating and they have a zero tolerance for that."

I couldn't have been more surprised to discover Lori harbored so much animosity toward Annie. I had wondered if there was some connection between them, but never imagined it went so deep.

"Uh, I'm so sorry to hear about this Lori." This was huge, but so many years later, why would she murder anyone?

"How is your brother, dear?" Dee Dee wiggled around in her chair like a bear trying to scratch an itch.

"He finally pulled himself together, took some classes at the community college and appealed for the university to award him his degree. They gave him an F in her class, but he eventually got his diploma."

Drat. I didn't like to think my freedom depended on pinning the murder on someone else, but it was my neck that would be in the noose so to speak.

She seemed spent after her rant. "Look, I shouldn't have told you all of this. I've tried to let it go, but it took my brother years to get over what she did to him." She shook her head. "When I found out she was going to teach this class I figured it would be the perfect time to confront her."

"Did you ever tell her about Leonard?"

"I know what you're thinking, but I didn't kill her. I didn't even get the chance to talk with her. I'm not sorry she's dead, but I didn't do it." Her eyes widened and she turned a shade paler. "You're not going to tell the detective about this are you?"

Boy was she delusional. "Lori, how about I give you the chance to tell her first. Then I won't have to." I wondered if I was giving a killer reason to go after me.

Dee Dee looked at her watch. "I think we need to go, Trix." She was giving me an out and I wasn't going to waste it.

I looked at my watch, too. "I believe you're right. We need to get back and check on Nana." I turned toward Lori, "my great-aunt Nana fell and broke her arm. We left her at the hotel by herself and we don't want to leave her alone too long. Thanks for talking with us."

"I hope you'll consider my suggestion not to tell Detective Sams what I've disclosed to you. I wish I hadn't spilled my guts but I needed to talk to somebody." Wow, had I put Dee Dee and myself in harm's way now? The soup and salad I'd eaten for lunch now felt like a lead ball.

"Okay, well thank you for your time Lori and we'll be on our way." Dee Dee grabbed my arm and pulled me toward the door. She didn't have to pull hard, because I harbored no desire to linger.

CHAPTER NINETEEN

We high-tailed it to the car. "Wow, she has a burr under her saddle," Dee Dee said. "Do you think she did it?"

"Yeah, I sensed she knew Annie, but had no idea she harbored such hate." I swerved to miss a car drifting into my lane. "Sheds light on Annie's attitude."

"You'd never kill over jealousy would you?" Dee Dee said. "I've heard of being bitter, but to lash out at someone for their talent, that's harsh."

I swerved to avoid a car speed-changing lanes.

"You'd think this was the Indie 500 the way people are driving. I don't know why everyone is in such a hurry," Dee Dee said.

"Holiday shopping traffic. It's only a couple more weeks until Christmas." I thought of how quickly the year had flown by; a year of being Mrs. Beau Beaumont. I wanted, no needed, to hurry home to him. I applied a little more pressure on the gas pedal.

"And here we are smack dab in the middle of a murder investigation. How did we get so lucky, Trix?"

"Don't know, but we have to find a way out of the middle. I can't wait to get back to work on the Ghoston article and home to Beau. I miss him." I could at least call and hear his voice, but I dreaded telling him about the murder.

"I wouldn't want to be in your shoes when you tell him about Annie. I wish he wasn't halfway across the country so he could help us." Dee Dee rooted around in her bag.

"What ya' looking for, Dee?"

She pulled out something, raised it in the air and yelled, "ta da! It was a pack of crackers. "My chicken salad has flown the coop." She held the package in front of my face. "Want some?"

My vision obscured, I slammed on the brakes. Thank goodness we were on a side street. I glanced in the rear view and let out a breath of relief since there were no cars behind us. "What in the world were you doing, Dee Dee. You almost got us killed."

"Sorry, I was just being nice. If you don't want any just say so."

"Uh, I didn't say that. Hand me over a couple, I could sure use some sustenance." She pulled two out of the pack and handed them over. "Yummy, cheese on wheat. Thanks, Dee." I didn't realize how hungry I was until I started eating. The crackers just whetted my appetite.

"What do you want to do for supper?" The thought of food was never far from Dee Dee's mind.

"I don't know right now. Give me a little time to think about it. Maybe we can look at the Chattanooga directory in our room and pick out a good restaurant." I'd thumbed through the directory earlier and noticed it listed dining choices, tourist attractions and accommodations.

"Sounds like a plan. I think I'll take a little snooze before we go out. I wonder how Nana's doing. She's something else isn't she? I hope I have the energy she does when I reach her age. Oh shoot, I don't even have her energy now." We both laughed at Dee Dee's observation. She was right though, on a good day Nana could run circles around both of us.

When we entered our room, Nana was talking on the phone. Now the proud owner of a cell phone for seniors and she loves to talk on it. I mouthed "who are you talking to?"

"Your mama. Want to talk to her?" My mother came straight from the lineage of Job. That woman had more patience than anyone I knew. But even Mama needed a break from Nana now and then. That's why I didn't mind taking her with me when I could.

"Sure, I'd love to." Mama came to my rescue more than once. Watching Nana for a while was the least I could do for her. I laid my purse and coat on the bed and took the phone.

"Hi Mama. How are things in Vans Valley?"

"The question is how are things with you, Trixie? I've been so worried about you and Nana. Do you want me to come pick her up and bring her home?"

"To tell you the truth, I've thought about it Mama, but I think we're fine for now. Nana's resting most of the time." Well, some of the time anyway.

"Okay, you just let me know if you want me to come." I knew Mama would come faster than a snowman melting on a sunny day, but I'd wait until I was sure I needed her.

"How's Bouncer?" Mama took care of my border collie when I was out of town.

"He's fine. He misses you though and I have to encourage him to eat. I find myself clapping every time he takes a bite." The familiar sound of Mama's laughter made me homesick.

We talked a few more minutes before I gave the phone back to Nana. By the time I said goodbye, Dee Dee was already snoring. I didn't blame her. I'd love to take a nap, too, but I needed to get busy studying my research.

Nana wound up her talk and flipped the phone closed. "When's supper?" I couldn't help but laugh.

"We're going out later, Nana. Let Dee Dee sleep for a while and I'm going to work on an article. You know how Harv can be."

"I sure do. He's too hard on you. I don't know why he yells all the time."

"That's just his way. He's not really as mean as he sounds. I'll admit he's hard-nosed. He expects the best from his writers. He gets under my skin sometimes, but I'll never forget the chance he gave this rookie." I don't know what I'd have done without Harv. I owed him for taking me on when no one else would.

"Why don't you look through the Chattanooga directory and see if you can find us a good place to eat? Maybe somewhere we haven't been before."

"Sure, I can do that, but if we were at home and I didn't have a broken arm I'd be cooking up some fried chicken, mashed potatoes and homemade biscuits."

"Oh, that sounds good, Nana. I wish we were home right now feasting on one of your meals. In the meantime we'll just have to make do. I'm going to go through these pictures Tilly gave me. It's amazing all the information she'd accumulated. She kept newspaper articles from Bobby Lee Ghoston's murder and collected lots of pictures. Did I tell you she's the official historian for Lookout Mountain?"

"I believe you did. I think I'll walk around the lobby while you work."

"Do you think you feel well enough? You're not dizzy are you?" I was worried the effects of the pain medicine hadn't worn off.

"I'm fine. Don't worry about me."

Yeah, famous last words.

"Did you say something dear?"

I swanny, could she read my mind now? "No, Nana, you go ahead. I'll be through in an hour or so and then we'll go out for supper."

Nana donned her coat and scarf, grabbed the Chattanooga directory and headed to the lobby. There was a short walk outside before entering the main section of the hotel. I propped my pillow against the headboard and spread newspaper articles and photographs in front of me. How was I going to make heads or tails of all this?

CHAPTER TWENTY

I reviewed the information Tilly had given me on the Ghoston Murder. Bobby Lee and Tad had been friends since high school, and together they owned a furniture store in Rossville named Furniture Warehouse. Both of them were married, and while Tad and his wife had one child, Bobby Lee didn't have any.

Tad's wife left him alone to raise their daughter, Tabitha. It was a surprise to everyone when he suddenly died from a heart attack. Bobby Lee and his wife took in Tabitha and raised her like their own. Bobby Lee was found murdered in his warehouse. And Tilly said there were rumors and accusations that Bobby Lee was a member of the Dixie Mafia.

Next I read the newspaper articles on Bobby Lee's murder. They never found a suspect and they blamed the murder on a botched robbery since the body was found with his wallet contents strewed around him. I studied the pictures of both men. I thought Bobby Lee looked familiar, but the picture wasn't of the best quality, so I wasn't sure of what I was seeing.

I made a quick call to the furniture store, and found out it was still in operation. Rossville wouldn't be that far. Maybe we could take a trip and check it out. I couldn't imagine how I was going to work on two murders at once, but I didn't have a choice. I needed to prove to Harv I could handle whatever he threw my way.

I heard Dee Dee moving around. "Hey, girl, you awake?"

She opened one eye. "Barely."

I stretched my arms above my head and released a big yawn. I was ready to get off this bed and go out for a while. "Want to go find Nana and head out to eat? She's supposed to be in the lobby."

"Sure, give me a few minutes to freshen up."

"I'll go get Nana." I stretched out my knee, rubbed it and waited for the tendons to relax.

We chose the Southern Belle Riverboat cruise, and while they finished getting ready I managed to get us last minute reservations.

We drove through town, enjoying the light display, and parked close to the pier. A fishy smell permeated the air. After walking down to the dock, our coats pulled tight against the chill, we stood in front of the three story riverboat and stared in awe. Inside, we were greeted with the eloquence of a five star restaurant.

The hostess seated us, along with other guests, at a long table. Several of these tables lined the room with the buffet in between them. A wooden dance floor made from walnut covered the rest of the room. A four piece ensemble sat in the corner.

"Wow, can you believe this place? I've never seen anything like it, but then I've never eaten on a riverboat before. I can't wait to get at that buffet." Nana eagle-eyed the feast laid out before us. Fried fish, baked fish and broiled fish dotted the buffet accompanied by sides such as slaw, hush puppies, greens, and cornbread to name a few. Cakes and banana pudding were offered for desserts.

"You're right, Nana. This was a wonderful idea. I'm so glad you found it. I wish we had dates so we could dance, too." Dee Dee looked at the dance floor. I expected her to break out in full swing any minute.

I knew as soon as the words left her mouth it was too late. Nana wasn't going to let a little thing like a date keep her from a night of dancing.

She looked around the room. "I see a lot of men we can borrow for a dance or two."

Oh, my goodness. Maybe this wasn't such a good idea after all. I had to admit I would have loved to have Beau's arms embracing me. A moonlight ride on a boat, with the one you loved, would be so romantic. I'd call Beau tonight barring any catastrophe.

"Nana, we can't do that."

"Why not Trixi? It might be fun." I could see I wasn't going to get any help from my friend. Nana had found an ally in Dee Dee.

We filed up to the buffet with the other guests. As people piled their plates full I couldn't help but picture pigs at a feed trough. I helped Nana with her plate since she only had one good hand. In between bites we talked with our neighbors as well as the couple from Cincinnati seated across from us. Nana kept everybody entertained while we ate. She held her arm up and invited everyone to sign her cast.

The band struck up a chord of "Let Me Call You Sweetheart," as couples made their way to the dance floor. Nana sang the words to the song and I could tell she itched to get on the floor. We enjoyed strawberry shortcake while listening to the band. Then it happened in the blink of an eye. Nana eyed her target. Before I could intercede she'd tapped the unsuspected dancer on the shoulder and cut in. I looked heavenward and asked for help. *Lord save me from dying of embarrassment, please.*

God must have been busy taking care of something much more important than my embarrassment. During the second song Nana decided to do the Charleston. Her partner slowly backed away as Nana danced the rag while the band played a lively tune. Quicker than a coon treeing a squirrel, the crowd formed a circle around her.

My breathing quickened and sweat popped out on my forehead. My vision blurred as I tried to focus on my great-aunt vying for the center of attention. I gasped for breaths expecting to pass out any moment. Dee Dee noticed my anxiety and grabbed my hand. "It's all right, Trix. She's having a good time and the crowd is enjoying her show." I didn't know whether to believe her when I heard a loud ring of applause. I couldn't believe my eyes. The crowd was clapping wildly for Nana.

Her partner, who'd acquiesced the floor to Nana, escorted her back to her chair. He gave her a little peck on the cheek. "Night ladies," he said, and returned to his previous dance partner. "Whew, I'm exhausted. Did you see me Trixie?"

"Yes, I saw you Nana."

"I told you we didn't need dates to dance." Nana waved at her fans as they passed by. "I'm so glad we decided to come here for supper. What an evening. Trixie I have to admit, you know how to show a girl a good time. There's never a dull moment when you're around."

Dee Dee guffawed at Nana's observation. I didn't think it was so funny. I looked around the room for an escape. I was ready to return to our cozy hotel room. While I surveyed the room I spotted a familiar face. My heart leapt into my throat.

CHAPTER TWENTY-ONE

Amanda Holbrook sat beside a woman, their foreheads so close in conversation they almost touched. Before I could look away, she noticed and pointed in my direction. The other woman looked my way. I poked Dee Dee. "Don't look now, but there's a woman over there, Amanda Holbrook, from my writer's class."

"We should go talk to her," Dee Dee said, and before I could stop her, she was headed over. I gave up resisting, and followed Dee Dee. Maybe the entire night wouldn't be lost.

Amanda's eyes widened as we approached. I thought for a minute she might bolt from the room. "Hi, Amanda. Do you remember me?"

"Of course I remember you. You were in my writer's class." She moved a little closer to her friend. "Aren't you the one Detective Sams spent so much time interviewing?"

I pulled Dee Dee closer. "This is my friend, Dee Dee Lamont."

Amanda gestured. "This is Bethany Smith. She encouraged me to get out and have a little fun. I never dreamed we'd run into you here."

"Well, I'm glad we did. I'd like to talk to you about Annie's death."

"You mean her murder," Amanda said.

"Yes, Detective Sams stated as much." I had this strange feeling I'd seen her somewhere else. I just couldn't place where. "Have we met before?"

"No, I don't think so. What do you want with me anyway?"

"Look Amanda, the truth is, Detective Sams told me I'm a person of interest because I was the last person to be with Annie before she died. I'm questioning everyone in the class to see if I can discover some helpful information. Do you mind if we join you for a few minutes and ask some questions? You know, we have a lot in common. I had a no good, low down, scum sucking husband, too. I know what it's like to be betrayed by the one you love."

I must have hit close to home because her bottom lip quivered and her eyes pooled with unshed tears. "I never thought it would come to this. I gave him everything I had and he just tromped all over my heart. It's broken into so many pieces it feels like its being held together with Band-Aids." She looked me square in the eyes. "To tell the truth, if I was going to kill someone it'd be my ex-husband. I didn't have anything against Annie."

"Did you know Annie before the workshop?"

She averted her eyes. "No, no I didn't." She sniffed and wiped her nose with her napkin.

I got the feeling she was hiding something.

"Can you tell me anything about the evening of the murder that might help me?" Any tidbit of information could help solve the crime.

"Let's see. My room was down the hall from Annie's, but I don't remember anything out of the ordinary." Her eyes lit up. "Wait a minute, I remember hearing voices outside my door and I cracked it enough to see. You were in the hall with Tippi" – she made finger quotes – "with an i". You were discussing something, but I couldn't hear what. After that, I decided to work on my assignment. I went to sleep in the chair and didn't wake up until after midnight when I went to bed." Amanda's friend handed her a fresh napkin.

"I told the detective about seeing Tippi in the hall, but I wasn't sure she believed me. Now I have your word to back me up."

Dee Dee wrote feverishly, this was the first tidbit of information in my favor and Dee took her job seriously.

"One more question, Amanda. Do you know where any of the other participants are staying?"

"Actually I do. Bodene Tate informed me he'd be staying with a cousin of his. I believe his name is Bubba Tate and he lives in Rossville. Bodene was bragging about some invention his cousin made millions on."

"Do you mind if I ask where you're staying?"

"I-I'm staying with Bethany."

Bethany held out a business card for me. I gave my card to Amanda and urged her to call me if she remembered anything else or if she just wanted to talk. I recalled the loneliness I'd experienced after my divorce.

Nana was back on the dance floor with a new partner. I turned to Dee Dee. "After this dance we need to grab Nana and take off before she draws any more attention. I want to get back to the hotel so I can call Beau. I miss him so much."

"I know you do, Trix." A big smile appeared on Dee Dee's face, but it didn't reach her eyes.

"I'm sorry, Dee," I reached over and gave her a shoulder a squeeze, "You must miss Gary, too."

"I do Trixie, but I have to admit, since you've come into my life our adventures give me something to look forward to. And of course, I have Antiques Galore. We help each other."

"Isn't that what friends are for?" The band struck the last chord and the dancers clapped their appreciation. Nana returned, her face glowing. I swanny, she looked ten years younger. How did she do it?

"Whew, that was fun." Nana slipped off her shoe and rubbed her foot with her good hand. "The night is young."

"Nana, the night might be young, but I'm not. I feel like I've been run over with a monster truck. I think we need to call it a night." I looked at Dee Dee and winked.

"Have you got something in your eye, Trix?" I should have known better, I've tried this trick several times with Dee Dee and it never works.

"No, Dee, I don't have anything in my eye, but my eyeball." I'd try the direct approach. "Don't you think we need to call it a night?" The light bulb finally flicked on.

"Oh, yeah, that's right, I'm bushed." Dee Dee stretched and yawned playing the part well.

After returning to the hotel it wasn't long before Nana faded out. I went into the bathroom seeking a little privacy, making the long awaited call to Beau. At the sound of his voice, my stomach did a somersault.

CHAPTER TWENTY-TWO

"Hi, Babe. How are you?"

The waterworks poured, "Oh, Beau it's terrible." So much for not worrying him.

"Trixie, what's the matter. Tell me what's *terrible*." My heart broke at the sound of his concern.

"You're not going to believe what happened. Please don't be mad at me." I dreaded telling him I was the main suspect in a murder case. Would he abandon me like Wade?

"Honey, I'm not going to be mad unless you don't tell me what's going on. Is everyone all right? Is Nana okay?"

Beau loved Nana like his own aunt. I couldn't prolong his agony any longer. I reached over and grabbed a wad of toilet paper and blew my nose. "Beau, I'm a person of interest in a murder case." I thought I'd soften the blow by using that expression. Being in law enforcement, though, it didn't fool him.

"You're a suspect in a murder case? How? Why?" Beau sputtered, hardly able to get his words out.

"I found our teacher, Annie, in the deep freeze. I didn't mean to." Well, what a stupid thing to say, of course, I didn't mean to. The words poured as I told Beau the story. "I was hungry and I went downstairs to get something to eat. I found a pink sash hanging from the freezer door so, of course, I wanted to see what it was. Beau, it was attached to Annie." The tears flowed again.

"Babe, that's horrible, but finding the body shouldn't land you on the suspect list.

"I wish it were that simple. Detective Sams, she's the lady detective on the case – you ought to see her Beau – she's Dee Dee's twin except for her skin tone. Anyway, she said they found my fingerprints on her teacup and teapot. Of course they did. I visited her earlier in the evening and she asked me to look at the set. My fingerprints were all over them. On top of that, I was the last one to be alone with her." I grabbed a fresh wad of paper to wipe my eyes.

"Slow down honey, let me think about this. What does the teapot have to do with anything?" I knew his criminal justice mind was working overtime and hoped he could piece together the facts so I could prove my innocence.

"Detective Sams said they found poison in her tea. Oh, I forgot they found some of the tea in my room. It's a rare blend of tea that she ordered off the internet. Beau, I think I've been framed. I don't have any other explanation for the tea showing up in my room."

"It sounds that way to me, too." He paused a beat. "You do need to prove your innocence."

At the same time as his comment made me feel better, it also set my heart to a panicked flitter. I'd hoped he would reassure me that it didn't look all that bad, but now he was agreeing I was in real trouble.

"Let me make some calls for you, and as soon as I can get someone to cover, I'll come over there and do what I can to help. It might take a day or so."

"I'd really appreciate that, honey."

"How's Nana taking all this?"

"You know Nana, she's ready to take on the world for me. She fell night before last and broke her arm, but she's doing great. She's sporting a hot pink cast and asking everyone to sign it." She wouldn't have any room left before long. "She even asked the waitresses to sign it. I've never seen anyone so proud of a broken arm."

The door squeaked open a little. Speaking of Nana, a little gray head peeked around the frame. "Trixie, you finished in there? I've got to use the lady's room."

"Just a minute, Nana, I'm talking to Beau." Oops, I spoke before I thought.

"Beau! Let me speak to him." She threw the door wide open. There she stood decked out in her footy pajamas.

I heard Beau's voice drift from the phone. "Trixie, is that my best girl?" He called Nana his best girl and she loved the nickname. That's how I met Beau. He was Mama's next door neighbor and helped her out with yard work, and when Wade stepped out on me, she invited Beau over for barbecue ribs and potato salad, and told me to bring a lemon meringue pie, and the rest is history.

He'd always been a help to Mama and Nana long before I'd moved back home. I'd forever appreciate what he'd done for them. And that was just a small indication of what kind of man my Beau is. I listened to the two catching up.

"Hey, Beau. You ought to see my cast. Sure, I'm doing fine. Can you believe the mess Trixie's gotten herself into? Don't you worry one little bit. Dee Dee and I are going to help Trixie find the real killer. We've already interviewed a couple of people and have more lined up. What? Oh, I love you, too. You want to speak to Trixie now." Nana handed me the phone with a smile plastered on her face. You'd think she was the one married to him.

We talked a few more minutes with Beau assuring me he'd come to Chattanooga as soon as he could. "Everything will be okay. God only knows why you're a magnet for dead bodies." I could hear the worry in his voice even as he spoke encouraging words to me.

I went into the bedroom and let Nana have the bathroom. Dee Dee propped up on her elbow. "What's going on?" She looked at Nana's empty bed. "Nana, okay?"

"Yeah, she's in the bathroom. I just finished talking to Beau. He'll be here in a few days."

Nana returned. "And I told him all about how you and I were gonna' help Trixie." A smile crept across her face. I failed to see the humor.

"Good for you, Nana. I'm sure he felt a lot better knowing you and I were on the case." Talk about being facetious. Dee Dee won the prize.

I yawned, then Nana copied me. "It looks like these detectives better get some shut-eye if we're going to get up early and interview Bodene tomorrow." Within minutes I heard a symphony of snoring, but I couldn't sleep. The glowing red numerals on the clock read one, and I still tossed and turned.

CHAPTER TWENTY-THREE

I dozed fitfully all night. Images of Detective Sams, Sergeant Gary Sargent, elves, and Annie in her pink bathrobe danced in my head. Nana's voice invaded my dreams. "Get up, Trixie. The sun's already up." Why was she telling me to get up? Then I felt someone shaking me. I waded through the thick fog of sleep and realized Nana was not part of my dream.

"What is it Nana?" I peeped at her with one eye.

"Come on lazy-head. It's eight already and you're not even dressed."

Nana was decked out in a matching ensemble. She wore hot pink jogging pants and jacket over a white tee shirt. I had to admit she was cute. Fortunately, her cast came to just below her elbow making it possible for her to dress herself. She must be feeling a lot better.

"Naaaana. It's too early to get up; I didn't sleep good last night." I pulled the covers over my head hoping she'd go away.

She pulled them right back off. "Oh no you don't. We have some detectin' to do today."

"Hey, what's going on over there?" Dee Dee sat up in bed. "My goodness, Nana, you're dressed already."

"Yep, we've got a job to do. We're not going to prove Trixie's innocence staying in bed all day." Nana put her hands on her hips and struck a serious pose. I couldn't help but chuckle, and Dee Dee joined in the levity.

"What's so funny?"

"Aw, Nana, you know we love you." Dee Dee tucked her feet into her kitty slippers, padded over and gave Nana a hug.

"Come on girls, get dressed so we can go get something to eat." This started another round of laughter. This time Nana joined in. It was good to laugh.

Less than an hour later we sat in an IHOP eating a stack of pancakes. I knew this wasn't the healthiest nutrition around, but it was comforting. I totally got *comfort food.*

I was pleasantly surprised when I found Bubba Tate's address. I called him up to ask if I could interview him on his invention. I filled them in while Nana dredged her bacon through a puddle of maple syrup. "He knew all about the magazine and was thrilled to be the center of attention." I felt bad for using him to get to Bodene, but I had to find a way to talk to him.

"What are you going to do if Bodene isn't there?" Dee Dee drizzled warm blueberry syrup on her pancakes.

"Let's just hope he is." I topped off my coffee and grabbed the sugary liquid. It looked delicious dripping down the sides of Dee's pancakes.

Our waitress approached the table. By the wrinkles etched on her face, she'd lived a lifetime and a half already, but she was probably only in her thirties. "I brought a fresh pot of coffee." She replaced the carafe sitting on the table." Is there anything else I can get ya'?"

"Dee Dee and I said "no thanks," but Nana asked for a couple more pancakes. Nana possessed a metabolism any woman would covet.

"Girls, we need to find a church to attend this morning. The Lord knows we could use all the help we can get. And I feel like the need for a good dose of spiritual food. " Nana wiped a drop of syrup off her chin.

"What a wonderful idea. We could stop at one on the way to Bubba's," Dee Dee said.

"I agree." We waited on Nana to finish her short stack and set out on our expedition. I was thankful for the short walk to the car. My new knee had taken more punishment the past few days than it had since surgery.

We followed the GPS towards Bubba's, looking for a church on the way. We weren't far from the Tate's when Dee Dee yelled. "There! It looks like we're just in time." Dee Dee read the name, "Southern Church of Faith, Deliverance and Restoration."

I swung a hard right and pulled into the gravel parking lot. There stood the classic Southern church building. An old wooden structure, painted white, with a steeple standing guard. A mountain of steps led to the double doors. I grabbed my camera from the car and took several shots.

As we climbed the steps, the strains of Rock of Ages drifted to greet us. I used the rail to pull myself up while Dee Dee assisted Nana. I opened the door to a sea of heads. The a cappella choir sounded like angels. If this was a rehearsal of heaven's welcome, then I couldn't wait.

A few heads turned as a young man ushered us midway up the aisle. A young couple scooted over to make room for us. We sang a few more songs before the preacher took his place behind the podium. About fifteen minutes into the sermon he nodded toward a couple of young men. They left only to return quickly with a long wooden box.

I nudged Dee Dee and whispered. "What is it?"

She shrugged. The preacher sprinted down front and opened the box. What was that rattling sound? Oh-my-goodness, recognition dawned like the morning sun. We'd walked in on a snake handling service. I looked at wide-eyed Dee Dee – she'd figured out what was in the box, too.

I grabbed her arm and squeezed. The pain in my chest felt like a hippopotamus jumping up and down. I looked around for an escape. I wondered if we could get out the door without making a commotion. I might just be going to heaven a little sooner than I thought.

The preacher held one of the snakes high overhead for the congregation to see. He continued preaching, something about having the faith to take up a snake, but I was faltering between planning my exit and keeping Dee Dee from moving more than an inch from me. Several people stood and headed down front. They each seized a snake from the box.

My heart beat faster than a jackhammer. Dee Dee tried to pry off my fingers from her forearm, but I wouldn't let go, my deathly fear of snakes paralyzed me. When I was growing up our neighbor had lost one of his fingers to a copper-head bite. He never overlooked a chance to show me his missing finger and tell me the story – over and over again. Thanks to Mr. Beadle I would forever be frightened of the slithering reptiles, no matter the species.

The leader cajoled again, "Who else has the faith? I feel it. There are others with us today that have the faith to embrace this wonderful creation of God." He held the wriggling reptile overhead and I swallowed, hard.

Events took a turn for the worse when I noticed Nana's empty seat. Where was she? I looked behind us to see if she was high tailing it out the door. No Nana. Surely she wouldn't do the unthinkable. Oh, yes, she would. I swiveled to face the front where the box was located. People, young and old alike, clapping and praising God, surrounded the wooden chest. The cluster of parishioners parted like the red sea and there in the center of the mass was Nana, grasping one of the snakes.

She shoved the serpent towards me as it wrapped a tail around her pink cast. "Here, Trixie, it's not so bad." I pushed Dee Dee aside, and held up my hands in protest. The last thing I remember was Nana's goofy grin as she thrust the slimy thing toward me.

Death came quickly.

CHAPTER TWENTY-FOUR

Okay, I didn't actually die, but I thought I had. If I'd really died and gone to heaven then Dee Dee went with me, because when I came to, her face was the first thing I saw. I pushed myself up to a sitting position. "What? What happened?" Full of cotton, my brain couldn't grasp the situation.

"Uh, Nana decided to get the spirit and take up a snake." Dee Dee warily eyed me and put her arm around my shoulder for support.

Memories flooded my mind. "Nana?" I looked around in hopes of seeing her alive.

She appeared beside me, and grabbed my hand in hers. "Here I am sweetie. You just passed out. Maybe the stress of being a murder suspect finally took its toll." There was a gasp from the crowd. They backed away as a unit. *Thanks Nana.*

I sat there a few minutes to get my bearings. I was thankful Nana was all right, but the feelings I harbored toward her didn't belong in church. As soon as I was able to stand I grabbed Dee Dee for support, and made my way out the door. Nana was still waving to her new friends as we walked to the parking lot. I couldn't get to the car fast enough. I slammed the door and engaged the lock. Nana hopped in the seat, apparently unaware of my anger at her.

"Can you believe that, Trixie? Did you see me hold that rattler? I knew the spirit picked me to tame one of those snakes – I felt it in the pit of my stomach."

"Probably gas," I mumbled. I'd wanted to experience a peaceful time of worship, but instead I'd been thrust into one of the most uncomfortable situations I could have imagined.

"Did you say something Trix?"

"Uh, I said we are going to be late for our appointment if we don't hurry."

Dee Dee glanced over at me. "You okay?"

"I'm just glad we got out of there with our lives."

"Now there you go again," Nana fussed from the back seat. "Maybe snake handling isn't how you want to spend your Sunday morning, but I see it as a sign from God that we can do all things."

"Maybe you're right, Nana," I said, "but I would have preferred a couple of traditional hymns and a relaxing sermon." I was beginning to see that perhaps Nana had a point.

"You sure looked confident up there," Dee Dee said to Nana. "If I didn't know better I would have thought you had experience with those things."

"I'm used to tossing aside garden snakes all the time, they're not so bad," Nana said. "Beau says they're good for the circle of life, dontcha know."

At the mention of his name, I felt a genuine peace, and thought of how God had answered my prayers for a godly man who loved me. Even if Nana's ways of worship didn't match with my own, her faith had reminded me I could look to Him in times of need, and I took in a couple of lungs of air, and decided to focus on finding the last bits of evidence that would clear my name.

But it was going to be a game of hide and seek, because all afternoon, the GPS took us in circles and no matter what route we took we came to a dirt road with crevices large enough for my car to disappear into. "Oh-my-goodness, what are we going to do?" I looked at the perilous road that stretched before us and cringed.

"Aw, come on, Trixie. Don't be a wimp. You can do it. Just go around the holes." Easy for Nana to say; it wasn't her car and she wasn't driving. But if I wanted to get there I didn't have a choice. Not according to the GPS anyway.

I inched forward precariously. At this rate it would take us an hour to reach our destination. I sped up a little and dodged to the right and then to the left. My stomach churned like a washing machine off balance. My nerves were stretched like rubber bands, and by the time we arrived at the end of the road Dee Dee had to pry my hands from the steering wheel.

We turned to pass between old tires, painted white. Half buried, they lined the driveway on either side. I wasn't prepared for what I saw next. Reminding me of a showy bridesmaids dress, there stood a two-story, colonial, brick home boasting large columns across the front, and huge turrets at either end. I glanced over to see Dee Dee's mouth hanging wide open.

Nana sat on the edge of her seat literally bouncing with excitement. "Oh, look at those beautiful statues."

In the center of the front yard, sculptures of David and Venus, painted skin-toned and topped off with yellow hair, screamed tacky. A gazebo stood between them, decked out with hanging baskets filled with colorful plastic flowers.

Dee Dee leaned forward. "Geeze, what happened here?"

"It looks like someone had more money than they knew what to do with." Surely this wasn't the work of a professional landscape artist.

Dee Dee voiced my thoughts. "They should have used some of it to hire a landscape company."

"Come on, y'all. I think it's great."

Nana would. "Okay, here's the plan. I'm going to interview Bubba and then I'll make a smooth transition to Bodene. That is, I hope it's smooth." After driving all this way I hoped Bodene would be home. I wondered how he'd react to my questioning him about Annie's murder. I had my doubts when he'd declared, "I didn't kill nobody."

"Look at that." Two giant Rottweilers dashed around the front of the house in full bark. Nana locked her door. "Who's getting out first?"

Dee Dee nudged me. "You're the one asking the questions, don't you think you should go to the door?"

"No, I don't." About the time I was ready to back up and get out of there, out stepped Bodene's twin, big, burly, and tattooed. I didn't know who was scarier, Bubba or the dogs.

The closer Bubba got to the car, the more I contemplated slamming the gear in reverse. But then he flashed a big smile, showing off bright white teeth, putting me a little at ease. He knocked on the window and I rolled it down a smidgeon. I wasn't ready to get out just yet.

"Hey, y'all. I'm Bubba Tate," he turned to the dogs. "Shut up!" and back to us, a raggedy toothed smile back on his face. "You must be Trixie Beaumont?"

I nodded. The dogs circled, one lifted its hind leg on a wheel.

"Well, get out and come on in." He tried to open the door but I held it closed.

"Uh, could you put your dogs up first?"

"Ah, don't worry about Sugar and Cinnamon. They wouldn't hurt a kitten." He yelled again, and they retreated to the back yard. Sugar and Cinnamon, talk about an oxymoron.

He opened the car door for me, and then jogged around to do the same for Nana and Dee Dee. I'd never have guessed this bear of a man would possess such manners.

"Why, thank you sir." Nana's twang made her sound like she'd just stepped out of the old South. "You are such a gentleman."

"I try to be. Y'all come on in and set a spell. My wife Elvira made some lemonade and cookies." Thankfully Sugar and Cinnamon stayed in the back yard as we climbed the steps.

Bubba's mansion was filled with furniture right out of the seventies; wall-to wall green shag carpet covered the living and dining room. With the bright orange leather couch next to a grass green recliner, flowered wallpaper copied off some hippie's alternative lifestyle poster, and I knew if you looked up "early redneck" in the decorator's dictionary, this is what you'd find.

Contrasted with the explosion of poor taste, Bubba's wife Elvira was pretty, petite and welcoming. I couldn't have been more surprised when she opened her mouth and spoke. "Hi, welcome to our home. We're glad to have you visit." Her accent reminded me of my Ohio cousins.

She laughed with abandon, tossing back lovely, shoulder-length blonde hair. Her green eyes sparkled with merriment. "You're wondering where I got my accent. Especially with a name like Elvira."

Nana spoke her mind. "Well, dear, you have to admit you don't sound like you're from the south. Where are your roots?"

"My roots are right here, I was born in Macon. My dad's job moved us north when I was little, but I moved back to attend the University of Georgia. I always missed the south and couldn't wait to get home. I'm so glad I did or I wouldn't have met Bubba." She looked toward Bubba and gave him a sweet smile. I thought for a minute they were going to run slow-motion into each other's arms.

"That's right. I'm thankful to God my little Elvira came home where she belongs. Now, Trixie, what would you like to know about me?"

"I'm dying to know more about your invention."

CHAPTER TWENTY-FIVE

A few minutes later, we sat around a coffee table laden with lemonade and cookies. I took a swig of the sweet concoction and savored the cool liquid running down my throat, anxious to get on with the questioning, but knew as the guest certain rules applied. "This is delicious Elvira."

"Thank you; it's my grandmother's recipe."

"If you don't mind, Nana needs her rest, and we don't want to take up your entire Sunday." I indicated the recorder, and Bubba nodded, so I turned it on. Dee Dee prepared to take notes. "Whenever you're ready."

He clutched the recorder and held it close to his mouth. "Well, let me tell you how I made my first millions. I always dreamed of inventin' something. I tried my hand at several different things, but I just couldn't sell them. Then one day I approached the Home Shopping Network with my newest idea and they ran with it. You'd be amazed how many orders we got for my solar powered headlight wipers.

"We had a real rainy spring, and my sales went through the roof. Next thing I knew I had a best-selling book, Elvira helped me with it—and I became a regular host on the show. We're so blessed to have all these wonderful things." Bubba swept his arm wide. "Yes sireee, we are surely blessed. Ain't we Elvira?"

"We sure are, Bubba."

I could hardly remember the questions I intended to ask Bubba I was so surprised. It goes to show you can't judge a book by its cover. For the next half hour, Bubba expounded on his fame, and even offered to send me and Beau prototype samples of his newest invention, a solar powered barbecue rotisserie.

Nana had sat quietly but finally piped up. "Trixie, isn't it about time we told them the real reason we're here?"

What! Oh, Lord, please put a filter on Nana's mouth. She was going to get us killed. We knew nothing about this family. Their friendliness could be a ruse and Bodene could really be a killer.

Bubba's smile faltered. "Well, pretty lady what *is* the real reason you're here?"

"Trixie wants to question Bodene about that murder," Nana blurted.

Bubba turned to me. "Is that true, Trixie?"

"Uh, yes, I would like to talk with him, but I wanted to interview you for *Georgia by the Way* first. I promise I'll notify you as soon as the article's published."

"Did I hear someone talkin' bout me?"

I turned to see Bodene filling the doorway. I attempted to swallow the cantaloupe stuck in my throat.

"Hey, I know you. You're that lady from the writin' class. What do ya' want with me?"

"Uh, I just wanted to ask you a few questions Bodene. As you know, our teacher, Annie, was murdered..."

"Yeah, I know that. So what? You sayin' I killed her?" His stare bore into my soul.

I averted my eyes. Avoid confronting a bear in the woods...or a killer in the sunroom? "No, of course not. It's just that I'm a person of interest because I was the last one to be alone with her." I didn't want to disclose too much information in case he *was* involved.

I was grateful when Dee Dee decided to jump in and help, because I felt like I'd just taken off on the Dahlonega Mine Train at Six Flags Over Georgia without a seatbelt.

"We thought you might have some information that could help Trixie," Dee Dee said.

Bodene sat his huge frame in a straight backed chair directly across from me. "Are you askin' me just because I was accused of killin' my ex?" He leaned forward, hands on knees, daring me to accuse him of killing someone.

"Uh, no. I don't know anything about your ex-wife." Surely the detective knew about this, but if not I couldn't wait to share my information with her. I knew she'd be upset I'd been to see Bodene, but what was this he was doing? Confessing or threatening? Or both?

Bubba jumped in, defending his cousin. "That's right Trixie, Bodene wouldn't hurt a fly. When Bodene's ex-wife was killed, the police arrested him. He waited in the slammer for a year before his case came to trial. He was found not guilty."

"Because he didn't do it, or because there wasn't enough evidence against him?" Nana gestured with a half eaten lemon cookie. They stared at her. "What?"

"I didn't kill nobody. They arrested me because I was handy. They didn't even try to find the real killer. Whoever kilt my sweet Lydia is still out there!"

Elvira poured him a glass of lemonade and patted his broad back. "I've encouraged him to write his jailhouse story, poor man. It might help clear his name with the people who still believe he's guilty."

Dee Dee furiously scribbled, and Nana jumped up, holding her cast aloft. "That sounds just like Trixie's story. She didn't kill Annie but she's being framed for her murder. Y'all have a lot in common. Maybe you could help her Bodene."

Bodene didn't seem convinced. "I wish I could help, but I don't think I recall anything from that night that'll help ya'. I went up to my room and worked on my writin' until I fell asleep." He ran sausage fingers through his wooly hair. "I'm sorry."

We were being dismissed, so I turned off the recorder, and thanked Bubba and Elvira for their hospitality. "If you recall anything at all, I'd appreciate hearing from you." We said our goodbyes and headed back to town. The spitting cherubs of Italian marble in my rearview mirror were a welcome sight, I'd had enough of backwoods Bubba and Bodene for a while. I was never so glad to be on Highway 27 heading back to Chattanooga.

"What do you think, Trixie?" Dee Dee worked in her tablet. "Looks to me like he's as good a suspect as anyone. How do we know he didn't kill his ex-wife? And that Elvira seems to be an odd one to be involved. What's she doing mixed up in all this?"

"I'm more confused than ever. I think I need to check in with Detective Sams. I know she's going to be upset, but I want to tell her I have a bad feeling about all this."

"If anyone wants my opinion I think they're a nice bunch of folk. I love their house and yard. I'll have to tell Betty Jo so she can decorate her flower garden with statues." Why wasn't I surprised Nana was infatuated with the Tate's?

CHAPTER TWENTY-SIX

Famished, we swung into Checker's drive-through for some burgers and fries. A hefty dose of grease and salt calmed my nerves considerably. When we returned to the hotel, we unanimously voted to take a nap. Uncooperative thoughts kept me from falling asleep, so I made a mental checklist of suspects we hadn't questioned yet.

We hadn't spoken to George, Tippi or Ladonna. I didn't know where they were staying and contemplated how I'd get the information. Before I could come up with a plan, I faded into dreamland. When I woke up, Dee Dee sat propped up against the headboard reading "Cowgirls Don't Cry." Nana snored softly.

"Must be a good book. Maybe I'll borrow it when you finish."

"It's a sweet romance. You'd enjoy it." She placed a bookmark in between the pages and laid it on the bed. "I called Stephanie while you were sleeping to check on the babies."

Ever since a cat decided my back was a landing pad, I'd been wary of the furry animals. I just didn't trust them. I tolerated Dee Dee's cats because I cared about her. "How are they doing? Are they missing their mama?"

"Trixie, I know you don't like cats, but you'd love my new baby. Have I told you about Whiskers?"

"No, I don't believe you have," I fibbed. If there was one thing I could do to repay Dee Dee for being the best friend I'd ever had, it was to listen to her cat stories. "Tell me about him."

"He's the cutest thing. Old Mrs. Bates came in the store the other day and told us about a little kitten that needed adopting. Knowing my love for cats she thought of me right away. As soon as I saw him I couldn't resist. He's black and has a little white stripe down his face. But that's not the cutest thing about him."

She rearranged her pillows and sat up a little straighter. "The mother left him, or maybe she was trapped or killed, but he still wants to nurse. He sucks on my fingers. Now isn't that the sweetest thing you've ever heard?"

"Uh, yeah, that is sweet, Dee. Are you going to keep Whiskers?" I stifled the urge to roll my eyes.

"I sure am. He's like one of the family now."

Nana sat up. "What are y'all talking about? I thought I heard somebody was sucking on Dee Dee's fingers." She raised her eyebrows.

"I was talking about my new kitten, Nana. He still wants to nurse."

"Oh, thank goodness. I thought it was somebody you were dating." Nana cackled at her little joke. Dee Dee joined her and before I knew it, I was laughing, too.

"I want to talk with Detective Sams, but she's probably not in the office on Sunday. I'll try first thing in the morning." I headed to the bathroom to freshen up.

"Let's do something fun. How about going to the Tennessee Aquarium? I've heard it's a wonderful place to visit and we could use a break. We could start our questioning again tomorrow," Dee Dee offered.

"That's a great idea. Don't you think so, Trixie?"

Somehow it just didn't seem right to go sightseeing while I was a suspect in a murder case. But I couldn't talk to the detective and I didn't know how to get in touch with George or Tippi, so why not have a little fun. "Okay, let's do it."

"All right!" Nana hopped out of bed and beat me to the bathroom. Dee Dee grinned from ear to ear.

The rest of the evening passed without incident. We grabbed a sandwich and chips at the aquarium deli for a late supper. I slept fitfully, my slumber filled with bizarre dreams. I was glad when Nana sounded the morning alarm.

"Rise and shine girls. Time's a wasting." Nana was already dressed in a teal green jogging outfit. "Let's go. We have a murder to solve."

Dee Dee pulled the covers over her head. If I had to get up she did, too. I took aim and threw my pillow onto her huddled form.

Dee Dee grabbed the pillow and took aim. A knock at the door interrupted her retaliation.

Giggling, I jumped up and opened the door, "Mama!" I flew into her arms. "It's so good to see you. What are you doing here?"

"I couldn't sit home one minute longer worrying about you girls." She came in, shrugged off her coat, and gave Nana and Dee Dee a hug. "Nana, how's your arm? Does it hurt?"

Nana held up her pink cast. "Aw, it hurts a little, but not enough to keep me from helping Trixie solve another crime."

"Trixie, what are you going to do?" Mama looked like she'd aged ten years since the last time I saw her. I hated being the object of her concern. I'd given her enough to worry about since moving back to Vans Valley. When I'd married Beau a weight lifted from her shoulders, now I'd gone and gotten myself into another mess. I seemed to be a murder magnet.

I threw on a pair of khaki's and a red pullover sweater. Dee Dee wore jeans with a blue sweatshirt covered in a snow scene. She carried an oversized Laurel Burch purse to match.

We ate pastries at the Café Espresso located in the lobby. I managed to get Mama alone and asked her to keep Nana busy, while I visited with Detective Sams. Nana wasn't happy, but she acquiesced. We planned to meet back in the lobby later in the day.

"Hey, Trix. Do you want me to give you a break and drive?"

Dee Dee's driving usually left me ready to kiss the ground when we arrived at our destination, but it was too tempting to pass up. "Sure, why not live dangerously?"

"Aw, come on, Trixie my driving isn't that bad." She offered me a knowing smile. "Where to first?"

"Let's head down to the police station and talk with Detective Sams. I hope she's receptive." I was happy we arrived at the station without a mishap.

A young blonde with short spiked hair sat behind the desk. She entered data in the computer like a pro. She looked up from her work and smiled.

"How may I help you?"

"Is Detective Sams in? I need to talk to her," I said.

Dee Dee nodded in agreement.

"She just came in. Let me tell her you're here." She asked our names and walked into the detective's office.

Before we'd settled in our seats, Detective Sams followed the officer back into the room. "Hi, Trixie. Come on in." Dee Dee tagged along. I appreciated her support more than she'd ever know. Then again, I was there for her when she was falsely accused of a murder in Dahlonega. She understood what it meant to have a true friend who would stand by your side no matter what.

The detective sat in an old swivel office chair. It squeaked in protest when her ample bottom hit the seat. I couldn't get over how much she reminded me of Dee Dee. It was obvious they saw the resemblance, too, by the way they studied each other. "Hello Ms…"

"Lamont," Dee Dee filled in for her. "But you can call me Dee Dee."

"Okay Dee Dee." She looked at me. "Is there something I can do for you? You here to give a confession?"

Yeah, right. "No ma'am. I'm here to offer my help." Oh-my-goodness, now I sounded like Nana, and I imagined Detective Sams thought I'd be as much help.

She confirmed my suspicion when she sat back and laughed out loud. When she saw that we weren't laughing she leaned forward and placed her arms on her desk. "You're serious."

"She's serious," Dee Dee said. "We've already talked to several of the people who were in Trixie's class and she has some information she'd like to share. She helped solve three murders and I'm sure she'd be an asset to your investigation." Dee Dee made it sound like I was a seasoned detective instead of someone who stumbled into murder scenes.

"Well, why don't you tell me what you've learned so far, then I can be the judge of that."

"Detective Sams," I had to stop to gulp back tears, "we've talked with Lori Wilson and she told us Annie failed her brother in college and kept him from graduating with his class. She didn't have any empathy for Annie. And Bodene was charged with his ex-wife's murder. Good grief, surely he's at the top of your suspect list."

The detective held up a piece of paper. "I have my list right here." She laid it back down. " And Bodene was acquitted of all charges against him. Like I told you, we're looking at everyone. Listen Trixie, I like you. My gut tells me you're not guilty of killing Annie. But the fact is, the evidence points toward you." She leaned back in her chair, one knee bouncing.

Dee Dee spoke up. "Don't forget to tell her about Amanda."

"What about Amanda?"

The young lady from the front desk stuck her head in the door. "Excuse me, Detective. I need to see you for a minute."

"I'll be back right back." The detective closed the door softly behind her.

Dee Dee grabbed her phone from her purse. "Keep a look-out, Trix."

CHAPTER TWENTY-SEVEN

"Why?" I had no idea what was brewing in that mind of hers.

"Don't ask questions, just let me know when she's coming back."

"Okay." I kept an eye on the door and listened for signs of the detective returning.

Dee hurried around the detective's desk, hitting her thigh on the corner. "Ouch, that hurt." She stopped to rub the painful spot and hurriedly took a picture of the paper containing the names of the other students. She no sooner sat back down when the detective walked in.

"Sorry about the interruption," she said. "I just got an update from the coroner's office. The poison found in Annie's body is from the Rhododendron family. She locked in on my eyes. I'm sure she was watching for a reaction from me, but the only one she got was shock.

I broke the stare under her scrutiny. "Why are you looking at me like that?"

"I just wondered what you knew about this." She didn't take her eyes off me.

"We don't know anything about killing somebody with flowers," Dee Dee said.

"She's right, Detective." Could this get any worse?

Detective Sams' body relaxed and she released her gaze as she changed the subject. "Do you want to tell me about Amanda now?"

I looked at Dee Dee, who nodded for me to go ahead. "We saw her on the riverboat the other night and she said her room was down the hall from Annie's. She heard my conversation with Tippi, confirming she was in the hall with me. Tippi could have been coming from Annie's room making her a likely suspect."

"Like I've already said, we'll be checking everyone out. I can't keep you from talking to the other writers short of arresting you, so I hope you'll watch your step. If the killer is out there, then they're not going to like you sniffing around for clues." Detective Sams stood up signaling she was through. "I suggest you stick to antiquing, or whatever brought you here."

"She came here to write a magazine article and got framed for murder," Dee Dee blurted. "No thanks to you she may lose her job—"

"Yes ma'am we will." I grabbed Dee's sleeve and tugged her toward the door. "Let's go, Dee Dee."

We made it back to the car, even though my knee protested every step in the dropped temperatures. "What were you doing with your phone?" I had gotten into the driver's seat. I needed to feel like I was in control of something in my life.

"You're going to love me for this, Trix. I took a picture of Detective Sam's list of suspects. And it has where everyone is staying. Who's your best friend now?" She grinned from ear to ear.

Oh my gosh, if the detective ever found out what Dee did, we were dead meat. But it wasn't like we were on her poker night invitation list in the first place. "You're going to paddle me further up the river." I jammed the key in the ignition and realized the information could save me from a lifetime in the big house. "Do not EVER tell Beau how you came to have these addresses, promise?"

"Pinky-swear." Dee Dee mimed turning a key to her lips, and threw it away. "Humm, it looks like Tippi's staying on the mountain and George is staying at the Sheraton Read House on Broad Street. Who do you want to drop in on first?

"Let's visit George first. I want to go back to the hotel and look through the pictures I have on the Ghoston murder. Something looked familiar to me in one of the pictures and I want to double check it."

"Okay, let's head on over to Broad Street."

The Sheraton Read House was located right down the road. It was an enormous old building and I couldn't wait to get inside and explore the historic structure. I remember as a child history bored me to tears. But since I'd been writing for *Georgia by the Way* I can't seem to get enough. I knew there'd be some great history behind this building.

"Look! That has to be it. Isn't it beautiful?" Dee Dee turned to the side to get a better view. Oh, I can't wait to see how it's decorated. It must be full of antiques. That reminds me, I need to call Sarah and see how the store's doing. I swanny I don't know how she keeps going at her age. I hope I have half as much energy as she does at eighty.

"Me, too, Dee." We opted to use the parking deck next to the hotel. "Do you think we'll have any trouble getting the number to his room?"

"Let's ask the desk clerk to contact George to meet us in the lobby. You can tell him you're from the magazine."

"Good idea." We walked the short distance to the elevator. As the doors opened into the lobby, I heard Dee Dee gasp.

"Would you look at this?" She stepped into the lobby and surveyed the huge room. "Can you spell opulence with a capital "O?"

She was right. Oversized chandeliers hung from the two-story ceiling in the atrium. Deep red couches and chairs were spread throughout the area, welcoming travelers. A concert grand piano graced the center of the room. The piano's reflection shone brightly from the marble floors.

I noticed a plaque showing the Read House was established in 1926. It wasn't hard to imagine the clientele of that time period. I pictured women attired in dropped waist dresses with a long string of pearls slung around their necks, their scandalous chin-length bobs turning heads.

Dee Dee nudged my arm. "Hey, close your mouth, a fly's going to take up residence."

"I don't remember when I've seen anything so grand." I did a three-sixty turn to soak up the décor.

"I know," she said. "I wish we had time to investigate, but we have work." Dee Dee pointed toward the reception desk.

The clerk behind the register smiled as we approached. "Your first time here?"

We nodded.

"Everyone is amazed the first time. Beautiful isn't it?"

Dee Dee returned his smile. "Yes, it is."

I could have stood there extolling the magnificence of the Read House all day, but if I didn't find Annie's killer, and soon, I'd be a guest in the big house.

CHAPTER TWENTY-EIGHT

"Could you tell me if you have George Buchanan listed as a guest?"

He checked his computer and curtly said, "Yes, would you like me to ring his room?" He indicated a small table with a house phone. "Or I can let him know you're here."

I nodded. "Well, would you tell him he has guests who would like to see him in the lobby?"

"Your names, please?"

"I-I'm a reporter for *Georgia by the Way*, name's Trixie Beaumont."

His smile grew wider. "Of course. If you'll take a seat over there I'll see if he's in." He lifted a handset, and we took a seat next to the piano, waiting to see if George would take the bait and talk to us. In less than five minutes the elevator doors opened and he stepped out.

"You." George didn't seem too happy to see me. "What are you doing here?"

I felt like saying, "I'm happy to see you, too Bubb," but I kept my snarky comment to myself. Any information George might have about Annie's murder was too important to mess up.

"As you know, I work for *Georgia by the Way*. I'd like to talk to you about Chattanooga. Since you write for a paper in the area, I thought you might have some information I could share with our readers." I crossed my fingers and hoped he'd respond. I felt kind of bad for using the magazine as a ruse for getting information, but I did plan on writing about Chattanooga and I'd use whatever he could offer.

"You know what, Trixie?" He shook his finger at me. "I don't believe you. I think you're here to question me about Annie. You want to save your own hide."

Busted, Trixie. "You're right George. I do want to ask you about Annie, but I intended to use any relevant information in my magazine article. I was just covering two bases at once." I looked around for Dee Dee so she could back me up. I saw her over by the piano lovingly stroking the slick surface of the beautiful instrument. Before I could say Steinway a security guard swooped in to caution Dee Dee.

I excused myself and hurried over to see what trouble she'd stirred up. I walked up just as I heard him say, "Ma'am we don't allow anyone to touch the piano. This is an antique and it's just for the pleasure of our guests. As you can see we have a sign saying "do not touch."

Dee Dee's face turned a healthy shade of pink. "I'm so sorry. I guess I missed the sign." She turned toward me. "This is my friend Trixie Beaumont and she works for *Georgia by the Way*," she said. "She's here to interview someone, and I was just admiring the antiques. I own an antique shop. By the way how did you know I was touching the piano? I didn't see you anywhere."

The security guard gestured toward a small camera in the corner of the ceiling.

"Sorry."

"I'm a bit of an antiques buff," the guard said, obviously charmed by Dee Dee's apology. "Have you seen the chiffarobe in the foyer? It's 18th century."

She turned to me. "Trixie, go ahead and conduct your interview. I'll be back in a while." She sashayed off with her new friend.

I turned around and was surprised when I almost bumped into George. I thought he'd probably taken the chance to retreat to his room. "Oh, you're still here." *Great deduction, Trixie.*

We talked a few minutes about his life in Chattanooga. Then I asked the burning question. "George, what can you tell me about Annie's murder? I know she wasn't very nice to you."

His voice raised an octave, "Not nice? That's putting it mildly. That woman humiliated me in front of the whole class. If she treats other people that way then I'm not surprised the old bat got what she deserved." Beads of sweat popped out on his forehead and his face scrunched up like a dried plum.

Why don't you tell me how you feel, George. "I'm sure you understand how important it is I find out who might have been capable of... well, fatally harming her?"

"I'll tell you this much. I saw the red-head going into that skunk's room that evening after class."

It was obvious he still harbored resentment toward our teacher. I wondered if he was angry enough to kill her. At least he'd confessed to seeing Tippi in Annie's room. I wasn't the only one who'd been in there. She could have easily spiked her tea. But why was he hanging around to see who was coming and going?

"Thanks for your help George. I'll pass this along to Detective Sams. I'm sure she'll find it useful." I hoped she would anyway.

I spotted Dee Dee getting off the elevator and hurrying our way. "Oh, Trixie, you wouldn't believe the treasures they have here." She turned to her companion and shot him a smile. "Daniel was kind enough to show me around."

Dee Dee seemed to have a way with the men. Every time we went out of town she struck up a new friendship, and she still emailed a few of them. It took a while after Gary died for Dee to even think about dating, but once she took that first leap, her social calendar stayed full. I enjoyed seeing her have so much fun.

Dee Dee watched Daniel stride away. "Isn't he a hottie tottie?" It didn't matter he was bald and had a little pooch. She watched him giving a couple some directions, and gave him a princess wave when he turned back to us.

"All right, man magnet, get your head out of the clouds and come on down to earth. We have a murder to solve." I couldn't help but laugh and she joined right in. Sometimes you just had to laugh to keep from crying and this was one of those times.

"Let's get back to the hotel and pick up Mama and Nana and take them out to lunch," I said. "Did you notice any places that looked good on the way here?"

"The English Rose Tea Room is directly across from the Chattanooga Choo-Choo. Let's try it." The parking deck offered a little shelter from the wind, but it was still cold. We hurried and got into the car.

"Sounds good to me." It was such a rush every time I turned the key to my P.T. Cruiser and it started on the first try. My prior car, a little red Jeep, ran on a prayer. After passing my six month probation period and working for Harv for a year, I'd felt secure enough to buy a decent vehicle. It still thrilled me to drive it. I only hoped I would have many more years of enjoying it, prison inmates don't have much use for a vehicle.

CHAPTER TWENTY-NINE

We called Mama and Nana to tell them we were on our way to pick them up for some lunch. When we arrived at the hotel I took the opportunity to grab the pictures for my Ghoston research. I wanted to confirm something that had been niggling at the back of my mind. We decided to bundle up and walk across the road to the tea room.

Dee Dee did a great job of picking a nice place. The English Rose Tea Room was enchanting. The delightful hostess seated us at a window table. A short history was printed on the front of the menu.

> *The English Rose was established in 1997 as an authentic British Tearoom, designed to bring timeless traditions of England to Chattanooga. The atmosphere, menu and staff reflect our British customs.*
>
> *The Tearoom is in the foyer of the original Grand Hotel. The hotel was built in the 1890's to accommodate passengers using the newly opened railroads to the South. This explains our location across from the Chattanooga Choo-Choo.*

"Isn't this charming, girls?" Dee Dee proudly asked.

"Yes, it is Dee," Mama said. "Why don't we get the Afternoon Tea? It sounds delicious. And it'll be on me."

"Aw, Mama, you don't have to do that." Dee Dee agreed with me and we bantered back and forth until we acquiesced. After all, Mama said we shouldn't deprive her of a chance to give. You can't argue with logic like that.

We told Mama and Nana about our adventure to the Sheraton Read House. Dee Dee couldn't wait to share about her new friend Daniel and what she'd seen. Everyone laughed at Dee Dee's tale of an argument they'd had over whether a chair was a Chippendale, until a maid overheard and showed them the Furniture Barn receipt. "I guess we were both a little twitter-pated," she admitted. Dee Dee knew her antiques better than I'd memorized my liver spots, so I knew she was falling quickly for Daniel.

While we waited for our scones, I browsed through the pictures. I studied the one that kept popping up in the back of my mind. I was sure the young teenager in the picture was Tippi. She was standing between Bobby Lee Ghoston and his wife. The red hair and the long legs caught my eye just like they did the first time I met her at the writer's workshop. Stunning.

I was eager to question her. Could an inheritance from Bobby Lee be a motive for murder? She did drive a fancy sports car. My mind was spinning with unanswered questions like a gerbil on a spinning wheel but getting nowhere.

"Hey, Trix, what's going on in that head of yours?" Dee Dee's question interrupted my thoughts. "You looked like you were a million miles away. Did you find something in those pictures?"

"Actually, I did, Dee Dee." I handed her the picture. "See the young girl in the middle?" She nodded. "I believe that's Tabitha, Tad's daughter and Bobby Lee's ward. Remember Tilly told us her story? The only thing is that she goes by Tippi now."

"If she was raised by the Ghostons, and stood to inherit a lot of money, then that's definitely a motive for murder," Dee Dee said. "Sounds like something we need to follow up on."

"Yeah, it does. I'm in!" Nana was sure she'd be invited along for the ride. I'd have to think quickly if I was going to get out of this. She saw right through me.

"Don't even think about leaving me behind, Missy." Nana crossed her arms as best she could with her cast.

I turned to Mama. "You might as well go with us." Maybe she could help keep Nana occupied.

"Honey, if you don't mind I'd like to go back to the hotel and take a nap. Now that I see Nana's fine I'd like to rest up. I haven't slept the last couple of nights worrying about y'all."

Dee Dee came to the rescue as usual. "Don't you worry about it Betty Jo. You go right ahead and rest and I'll help Trixie keep an eye..."

I interrupted before she finished her sentence. I didn't want Nana thinking Dee Dee was her babysitter. "Uh, that's right, Mama. We'll walk back to the hotel with you and get the car."

We finished our lovely tea, then got Mama settled in our room and headed up the mountain where Tippi was staying. We used the GPS to find the address Dee Dee had "borrowed" from the detective's desk. The house was gorgeous. It reminded me of a small mansion.

The brick home boasted two stories and a three car garage. Since land was scarce on the mountain, most of the homes had a small yard, but this home sat back from the road on at least two acres of land. It wasn't the opulent house that surprised me as much as seeing two police cars parked in front.

CHAPTER THIRTY

"Dee, what do you think's going on?"

"Looks like there's been trouble at the homestead," Nana said.

"I couldn't have said it better, Nana." Dee Dee unbuckled her seatbelt. She scooted up, sticking her head between me and Nana.

I pulled in the driveway behind the patrol cars. "My curiosity's killing me." *Probably not the best choice of words, Dee Dee.*

A poker-faced patrolman walked up to the car and motioned for me to roll down my window. "May I ask why you're here?"

The officer's nametag identified him as, Steve Smith. "Officer Smith, we're here to visit Tippi Colston."

"She's not here," he said.

I wondered how to broach the subject of finding out where she was when Nana piped up. "Well, where is she? We have an important business date with her and it can't wait."

"What kind of important business date?"

Way to go Nana. Open mouth and insert foot. But she wasn't finished yet.

"My niece is a murder suspect and she needs to question Tippi."

"That's right Officer. We're helping Detective Sams solve a case." I couldn't believe it. Dee Dee was getting as bad as Nana. They were determined to get me in trouble.

"You don't say? Stay right here a minute." He walked over to another officer. He turned our way and pointed toward the car. He walked back over.

"Ma'am, pull your car in behind the patrol car and y'all come with me."

I moved the car as told, then turned to Nana and Dee Dee. "Way to go girls. Now you've done it."

"Aw come on, Trixie, we just told the truth," Dee Dee said.

Officer Smith directed us to the back seat of his cruiser. "You ladies take a seat in here while I make a phone call."

The car had been running with the heat on and it was warm with all three of us squeezed in behind the iron cage. I felt like I was already in prison. I imagined he was calling Detective Sams to let her know about the murder suspect and her two accomplices running around questioning people. A bead of sweat rolled down my back.

Within minutes I saw the detective walking towards us. She didn't look happy. She beckoned to me to get out of the car. The fresh air felt good.

"I knew I'd see you again, but I didn't think it'd be this soon. Get your car and follow me to the station."

"You're in trouble now, Trixie," Nana said. *Lord please keep me from strangling her.* I loved Nana with all my heart, but that didn't keep me from getting frustrated with her at times. Before I knew it I'd rolled my eyes. Big mistake.

"Don't roll your eyes at me, Missy. I changed your diapers ya' know." I wasn't sure what that had to do with anything, but Nana never missed a chance to call me on eye-rolling.

Back down the mountain we went. Thank goodness there wasn't any ice on the roads. I couldn't imagine living on a mountain and being snowed in for days. I loved being able to get out too much. Loved my freedom.

The glittering Christmas decorations caught my eye. It was kind of hard getting in the Christmas spirit when you're suspected of murder. I had to find the killer and get this investigation wrapped up.

The same young lady was at the reception desk when we arrived at the office. She looked young enough to be in high school, and her spiked hair and a wad of chewing gum didn't help her image.

"I see you're back again." She smacked. "And you have a new person in tow." She looked at Nana. "Who do we have here?"

I could see Nana didn't take kindly to her condescending tone, so I stepped in. "This is my great-aunt, Nana. We're here to see the detective."

"She said to send you on in." Popping followed us as we traipsed into Detective Sams' office.

She stood up as we came into the room. Dee Dee diffused the awkward situation with a compliment on the detective's outfit, black pants with a red shirt covered by a Christmas themed vest. "Love your outfit."

The detective answered in kind. "I like yours, too." Dee Dee's outfit mirrored the detective's except for a white shirt. I felt like I was looking at the Bobbsey Twins.

Her friendly demeanor changed quicker than a duck on a Junebug. "What were you doing at Tippi Colston's? Were you there to question her on Annie's murder?"

"You told me you couldn't stop us from interviewing my classmates, so I decided to go ahead with it." My brazen answer startled even me, but I didn't have anything to lose and I was getting tired of all this. And why were all the police at Tippi's? Perhaps they were onto her as well. "George Buchanan said he'd seen Tippi Colston coming out of Annie's room earlier in the evening. This definitely gives us another person of interest."

"So then you went to Tippi's to question her?" Detective Sams said.

"That's right."

Dee Dee spoke my thoughts. "Did you arrest her for the murder, Detective?"

She looked from me, to Dee, to Nana. I wondered what she thought of our motely little crew. "No, we didn't arrest her. She's been shot. She's in Erlanger Hospital with a gunshot wound to her shoulder."

CHAPTER THIRTY-ONE

"What, how, why...?" I sputtered.

"Of course I can't divulge any pertinent information," Detective Sams said. "She's going to be all right though. That's the good news."

"I swanny they're dropping like flies around here. Sounds like being a writer can be a dangerous occupation." Nana walked over to the detective's desk. "By the way what are you writing in that little notebook of yours?" She leaned over and gandered at the tablet. "I hope it isn't anything about my niece, Trixie. You know she's going to solve this murder."

I could feel my face turning red. Being easily embarrassed had been something I'd dealt with since childhood. Hanging around Nana didn't help my condition.

"I don't want Trixie involved in solving this case. As you can see it can be very dangerous."

Dee Dee gently guided Nana back to her chair. "Detective, do you think the two cases are connected somehow?"

"We don't know at this time, but it wouldn't surprise me. That's why it's important you stay out of the way. I think the stakes have just been raised." She stood and walked around to the front of her desk and leaned against it. "Y'all can go now, but I want you to stay away from Tippi's house. It is now a crime scene." She turned toward me. "And I'll be checking with George about the information you gave me."

Okay, she left the path wide open for me to contact Tippi. The detective said stay away from her house. I had no intention of going there, but she didn't say anything about not going to the hospital. I didn't bring up the fact that I thought Tippi was really Tabitha. I'd find out for sure before I approached her with the information.

Detective Sams walked us out to the front room and reminded me not to leave the city. She made it clear I was still the main suspect in Annie's murder. What did this new incident mean? Was there a connection between the two women? I needed to get over to Erlanger and question Tippi. I knew Mama was resting, so I decided to take Nana with us. I hoped I wouldn't regret it.

Dee Dee grabbed my arm. "Why didn't you tell Detective Sams about the picture?"

"I wanted to give Tippi a chance to explain before I did."

"I hope she has a good explanation," Dee Dee said.

The GPS took us to Lee Highway then we hit Highway 27. It took us about ten minutes to arrive at Third Street. A sweet little gray haired lady sat behind the information desk. "Could you tell me what room Tippi Colston is in?"

She looked on the computer and wrote the number on a small piece of paper and handed it to me. "She's in room 424."

"Thank you." I took the paper and shoved it in my pocket.

"Isn't it about time for supper?"

Dee Dee's laughter echoed in the elevator. "Come to think of it, I could use a little sustenance."

"All right ladies, when we finish talking with Tippi, we'll pick up Mama and get something to eat." Nana responded with a smile.

We stopped on the second floor where a tall, dark, and handsome doctor boarded the elevator. Nana and Dee Dee giggled like schoolgirls as they ogled Dr. Hunky. Okay, I admit, I stole a quick peek, too. Dee Dee pulled out her hot flash fan and then they broke out in full laughter. The doctor turned around and smiled at them. I thought of Beau and wished he was here with me. He said he'd come as soon as he could – I hoped it was sooner than later.

The elevator stopped at the third floor and the doctor exited. "Girls, behave," I said.

"Aw, Trixie, we were just checking out the menu," Dee Dee said. "And I remember it hasn't been too long ago when you would have done the same thing. Just because you're married now doesn't mean Nana and I can't appreciate a nice dish." The girls broke into another gale of laughter.

"Touché." They had me there.

Nana shook a bony finger at me. "Yeah, if you hadn't hitched up with Beau I'd still be trying to marry you off."

"Well I did, so you can hang up your bow and arrow, Cupid." The elevator opened at the fourth floor and we got off.

We stopped outside Tippi's door. "All right, let me take the lead."

Tippi was lying in the bed looking like death warmed over. Her bright red hair accentuated her pale face. Dark circles beneath her eyes stood out like a wart on a pretty nose. She'd obviously been through a lot.

"Hi, Tippi." She looked at me and squinted.

"Can you hand me my glasses? They're on the bedside table." She put them on and the light bulb of recognition went off.

"What are you doing here?" The fire she'd shown the other day had been extinguished. "I hope it's not to gloat over my misfortune."

"Of course not, Tippi. I'm sorry someone shot you. Do you have any idea who it was?" I wondered if she'd tell us if she did.

"No. I don't. I have to tell you I'm scared. With Annie being murdered and me getting shot I wonder if they've targeted those in the class." She looked at me like she was seeing me for the first time. "Weren't you the last one to see Annie before she died?"

"Yes, she was. That lady detective's out to get her. She thinks Trixie's the killer." Nana just couldn't help but blab whatever thoughts were churning around in her brain.

Tippi's pretty blue eyes widened. "What do you want from me?"

"I need you to look at something and tell me if you recognize this young girl." She gazed at the picture and her eyes widened. I'd been right all along. Tippi was Tabitha Hopkins.

"It's you isn't it?" She nodded. "Why would you take on an assumed name?"

It's a long story," she said. "Everyone around Lookout Mountain knew my family. I'm sure you've heard the rumors that my dad was in the Dixie Mafia. Well, they weren't rumors – he was. When I decided to write for a career I took on a pen name. I didn't want to deal with the backlash of who my family is."

Dee Dee stepped in with her own question. "Did you know Trixie was writing an article on Mr. Ghoston's murder?"

"Yes, I did. Like I said, Lookout Mountain is a small area and news travels fast. I knew who you were the first day I met you at the writer's workshop."

"Is that why you were so...reserved?" At least there was a reason why she treated me like moldy cheese.

"Yes. I didn't want you stirring up old ghosts. The police suggested Bobby Lee's death was a botched robbery." She took a drink of water. "Maybe even somebody from the Mafia. I just wanted to get on with my life. I guess that sounds heartless, but I'd been through enough chaos over the years."

I didn't understand why she wouldn't want the killer of her guardian found and prosecuted. Mostly, I didn't think she'd killed Bobby Lee Ghoston, but there was a little niggle in the back of my mind that kept me wondering if it could have been her. She gained so much from his death.

We talked a little longer until the nurse came in and shooed us out of the room. It was obvious Tippi or Tabitha or whoever needed her rest. We left the hospital and traveled back to the hotel to pick up Mama. We decided to return to Sticky Fingers for supper. Mama hadn't been there before so it was a treat for her.

We discussed the latest events and tried to figure out who'd want Tippi dead. Did it let her off the hook if someone tried to kill her? Or was this someone warning her off from her newly discovered writing career? I tried to recall what she'd told me about her family being involved in organized crime, and chills ran up and down my neck. What had I gotten myself into this time?

CHAPTER THIRTY-TWO

As usual, Nana woke up before the roosters crowed. She was dressed in Christmas green jogging pants with a white turtleneck shirt. I just knew somewhere, there would be a green jacket to top off the outfit. "Let's go! Today's a new day and I've already made out a list of fun things to do to keep ourselves busy."

There was a chorus of groans. "Nana, it's not even eight yet. Can't we sleep in just one morning?" I wanted to pull the covers over my head and make this whole nightmare of a trip go away. But, I knew we'd never solve the case staying in bed all day so I gave up.

In a little over an hour, we were dressed and ready to face the day. A trip to IHOP for pancakes cheered everyone up. Nana pulled out her itinerary of fun things to do to take our minds off the seriousness of my situation. First on the list was the 3D IMAX Theater located next to the Chattanooga Aquarium.

There were two films playing. Nana chose the *Great White Shark*. We stood in line with rambunctious youngsters waiting to get in. Excitement shone on the children's faces as they fidgeted beside their parents.

Dee Dee suggested we get popcorn and Coke. So there we were, with our 3D glasses and refreshments, standing in line with the other kids. Mama and Nana had never been to a large screen movie. I couldn't wait for them to see the spectacular scenes. Finally allowed in, we flowed with the crowd to our seats.

The hostess appeared and provided us with interesting tidbits of information on the theater. It boasted the largest commercial screen ever invented. The IMAX screen is 4500 times larger than the average television and the screen is designed to include the peripheral vision.

The lights went down and the sound came on. Everyone scrambled to put on their glasses. The crowd gasped with wonderment at the beautiful ocean scenery. Colorful fish swam through the water as vegetation gently swayed.

I had to admit this was a great idea and I sat back to enjoy the movie. Next thing I knew a shark, jaws wide open, leapt from the screen into our laps. Nana jumped and popcorn flew onto her neighbor. Nana apologized, and blamed it on the shark.

We settled back and I was enjoying the movie when I noticed Nana's arms reaching out toward the screen. First they started slow, then they sped up and she was wildly swinging her arms. Nana's gesturing dislodged the glasses of the now disgruntled man next to her. I heard a few expletives from the irate movie-goer.

I laid my hands over Nana's for the rest of the movie and we made it through without any more catastrophes. When the lights came on the surly man shot daggers at Nana, but she only shrugged. "Sorry, I was really caught up in the reality of it."

Her apology diffused the tension and a smile appeared on his lips.

"Oh, that was so much fun. I'm so glad I added that to my list." I wished I had half as much spirit as she did. I glanced at Mama and noticed she looked like someone had stolen the color right off her face. She was as white as a newly painted picket fence.

"Mama, what's the matter?" With all the attention I'd been paying to Nana, I hardly noticed what mother was up to during the movie.

Dee Dee supported her from the other side. "Betty Jo, what is it?"

"I'll be okay. I just got a little seasick. Let me sit for a few minutes." We guided her to a bench. Nana sat beside her and grabbed her hand.

"Want some Coke, Betty Jo?" I could feel the genuine love between Nana and Mama. When her parents were killed, Nana took in Mama. Now that Nana's getting older, Mama's showing the same love and care for Nana.

"I think I need to go back to the hotel," Mama said. "I don't know what's wrong with me. I think I'll feel better if I can rest for a while." She looked so pale.

"The action and movement can cause queasiness, Mama, that's no problem. We'll be glad to take you back so you can lie down."

She straightened, but still held a hand to her forehead. "No way. I won't have you sitting with me. You take Nana and finish up that list of things she wanted to do. I'll hear of nothing else. I'll be fine."

"Are you sure, Betty Jo?" Dee Dee handed Mama a Coke and sat down on the other side of her. We gave her a few more minutes, then dropped her off at the hotel and tackled the next stop on Nana's list.

We were lucky to find a parking spot right in front of the Creative Discovery Museum downtown. As soon as we walked in, and I saw the hands on exhibits, I knew Nana would be determined to experience each and every one. Cute little twin girls stood beside her as they dug for miniature artifacts in the dirt. Nana squealed when she found a replica dinosaur bone. I wasn't sure which of them had more fun.

While she was busy, Dee Dee and I sat and talked. "Hey Dee! Look over there." Dee turned in the direction I pointed. "That's Amanda Holbrook with her friend we met the other night on the Riverboat," I said. They were next to a round cement bowl, I couldn't imagine what it was for.

It was odd to see them there. We hadn't run into any of my other classmates, but this was the second time we'd ended up in the same place as Amanda.

"I wonder if they're following us." Dee Dee said what I thought.

"Aw, probably not." I decided it was just coincidence. Why would she be following me?

CHAPTER THIRTY-THREE

As I said that, Amanda's head popped up and turned as if she'd heard me. Surely she couldn't have heard that from across the room. I was relieved when she smiled and waved to me and Dee Dee. Phew, that was close. We needed to be careful what we said in public. Especially while we were sitting right next to sound amplification exhibits. I waved back, and then grabbed Nana so we could move to a different room.

By the time we finished, it was lunch time. We chose to get a burger at the Big River Grille, where we discussed Nana's *agenda* and what we wanted to do next on the list. We bundled up before we went back outside. The sky was crystal clear, allowing the sun to shine like a bright copper penny warming the air. We couldn't have asked for a more beautiful day.

Next stop – Walnut Street Bridge. According to a brochure Nana had picked up, the 1890 bridge was the first to connect Chattanooga with the North Shore.

The bridge, closed to motor vehicles in 1978, sat in disuse and disrepair for nearly a decade. Repairs and structural modifications had been made to turn the bridge into a pedestrian walkway. The Walnut Street Bridge was added to the National Register of Historic Places on February 23, 1990. The 2,376 foot span is one of the world's longest pedestrian bridges, and sits near the heart of a massive and recently completed urban renewal project. The bridge is well loved by local residents and very popular among tourists. From December 2009 to May 2010, the bridge's deteriorating asphalt surface was replaced with wood planking. Tourists walked on both sides of the bridge stopping to admire the view.

The bridge, covered with fairy lights, is a photographer's dream when the sun goes down. I was glad I'd brought my camera from the hotel when we dropped off Mama to recover her tummy.

We were halfway across the span when we stopped to view an island in the distance. I was busy taking pictures when Nana said, "Watch this!" I knew whatever she was about to do couldn't be good. I'd heard the story too many times about the redneck's last words, "watch this!"

I turned to see Nana spitting off the side of the bridge. Dee Dee wasn't going to be outdone. "Let me try." Dee Dee leaned out and took her turn. Oh – my – goodness, how did I get so lucky to have these two for companions? "Come on, Trixie, give it a try."

"Have you lost your mind?" I'd done a lot of things, but spit off a bridge was not one of them. But those two had no intention of giving up.

"Trixie, surely you aren't too good to see how far you can spit." Nana's eyes twinkled as she threw down the gauntlet. "Life is too short to be so uptight all the time."

I wasn't going to let a little sprite of a woman get the best of me. "All right. If that's what you want, then I'll show you. I happened to be the neighborhood champion back in the day. I out spit all the boys." I readied myself and spit for all I was worth.

We crowded together to see where it would land. Unfortunately none of us thought about the boats that floated under the bridge. What were the odds that a riverboat crammed with people on deck would appear from under the bridge the same time my glob of spit careened in the wind? I could see a lady wiping her face and looking up. Then several of the surrounding people were pointing up at us. We backed up, and hurriedly walked down the bridge before stopping to catch our breath.

I was mortified, but a nervous giggle escaped my lips. "Well, I hope you ladies are happy now. I just hope no one recognizes me from that distance. I'll be in trouble for sure. Wait and see if I let y'all talk me into another hare-brained idea." *Lord, please send me some patience, now!*

Dee Dee gave my shoulder a thump. "You did win the distance contest, though!"

"And accuracy!" Nana added, and she and Dee doubled over in laughter. I had to admit it was funny, but I still felt awful for the poor woman.

"Come on Trixie, we're headed over to the merry-go-round on the other side of the bridge. I know that'll cheer you up." Dee Dee and Nana started discussing which animal they wanted to ride. I was grateful that for just a few minutes I'd forgotten about the murder. But there was nothing I could do until either Beau arrived, or Detective Sams found evidence to clear my name. I allowed Dee and Nana to lead me inside.

Thank goodness the merry-go-round was located in a large warm room. According to a plaque on the wall, the carousel was built in Atlanta in 1895 by Gustav Dentzel where it made many children happy until its dismantling in 1960. Several businessmen found it in a deteriorated condition and hired artists to refurbish it for use in Coolidge Park in Chattanooga.

It was unlike any other carousel I'd seen. There were not only the usual horses, but colorful, unique animals. A tiger, giraffe, elephant and a bunny decorated the carousel. The excited children ran around trying to decide on a favorite.

"Which one are you going to ride?" Nana was buying a ticket.

"I'm choosing one of the horses. Aren't they beautiful?" Dee Dee dug in her purse for some change. "Trixie, have you picked one out yet?"

I recalled a similar carousel I'd taken my daughter, Jill, on and it brought back fond memories. "I don't know, I'm going to walk around before I choose." How would Jill take it if her mama was convicted of murder? I was deep in thought when I heard Nana's shrill voice.

"No, I was here first." What was going on? I looked to see Nana and a little girl standing beside a giant gray bunny with pink ears.

The determined child stomped her foot. "I saw it first."

"Well, you might have seen it first, but I beat you to it."

I expected Nana to stick her tongue out any minute. Dee Dee came up behind me. "Oh, boy! I guess I need to referee." She grabbed Nana by the elbow and eased her toward a couple of horses. "Nana, come on, ride with me."

"All right, I didn't want to ride on a bunny anyway." I followed a few steps behind. As usual Dee Dee took one of Nana's capers and diffused a possible disaster. She mouthed, "Sorry," to the little girls' astonished parents as Nana climbed up on a chocolate brown steed. I'd be forever grateful for her help with Nana. "Come on girls, let's go back across the river," I said when the ride was finished, glad Mama hadn't been with us. The round and round motion had left me a little dizzy.

"Goodie, the museum's right past the bridge and that's next on my list," Nana said.

The quiet of the Hunter Museum of Art beckoned. I'd researched, and knew it was a blend of an historic mansion with a modern facility built on an 80 foot bluff overlooking the river. You could stand on the bridge and see the beautiful architectural creation. This is one place I really wanted to see.

I snapped pictures from one end of the bridge to the other. On the right side was the aquarium and on the left was the museum. I expected my article on Chattanooga to be a memorable one. Now all I needed to do when we got back to the hotel was to work on the Ghosten murder.

As we wandered from one exhibit to another, I thought about the case. Discovering Tippi was really Tabitha had given me a new direction to consider, but I couldn't quite fit the pieces of the puzzle together. While it was obvious Tippi stood to gain financially if she killed her guardian, I just didn't have the feeling she was the killer.

I had an idea about who framed me and probably killed Annie, and I'd check my theory out when I got Nana back to the hotel. As we enjoyed the museum, I wanted to go into the mansion part of the building before we ran out of time.

"Do y'all want to come and see the mansion owned by George

Thomas Hunter, a Coca-Cola bottling tycoon? The brochure says it was built in 1904."

"I'd like to go outside and look at the river from the bluff. You know they have those telescopes you can put a quarter in and see from here to yonder," Nana exclaimed.

"I'll go with her, Trixie, you go ahead and we can meet up later," Dee Dee offered.

I think she was giving me a chance to be alone for a little while. I decided to grab it. We agreed to meet in thirty minutes at the gift shop. Lost in the art, for a few minutes, I almost forgot I was a murder suspect. I discovered one of my favorite pieces of art, The French Tea Garden. I wished I could be transported into the picture and disappear from my troubles. But that was impossible so I would depend on God for my strength. *Father help me through this difficult time and direct my footsteps to the path of truth.*

I was soon to find out just how fast he would put my feet on that path. I strolled out on an open air deck to observe the beautiful scenery. The wind had picked up so I put on my coat and leaned against the rails. My thoughts flowed as freely as the river, when a dull object poked me between the shoulder blades.

"Don't move," a deep voice commanded, and this time it wasn't spit I thought would hurl over the railing.

CHAPTER THIRTY-FOUR

Instinct kicked in and I turned around. "Amanda? What are you doing?" I was right all along. Amanda was the only one absent from the room when we gathered for Detective Sam's talk. She had to be the one who planted the tea in my room. "It was you wasn't it?"

"Geeze, what gave me away?" She hissed. "If you want to stay alive you'd better do what I say. We're going for a little walk, so don't try anything." She slid a coat, thrown over her arm, up to cover the gun barrel. Motioning to the door, she shoved me inside.

We boarded the elevator and rode to the basement floor. It turned out to be a storage area with minimum light. Is this where she was going to leave my lifeless body? It took a few minutes for my eyes to become accustomed to the dark. Why had I come with her? If we'd stayed out in the open I might have stood a chance. But it was too late, and she had me in her lair.

Amanda stood in front of me, pink-handled gun clutched in her grip. I had to give her credit for being stylish.

Keep her talking, Trixie. "What do you want from me, I'm just an old lady?" I'd been watching cop shows with Beau, and he always had something to say about procedures done right or wrong by Hollywood. I wracked my brain to recall hostage situations. "I understand you're afraid, so let me go and I won't say anything." Good one, establish trust.

But Amanda ignored me. "I heard what you said in the Discovery

Center. And yes, I am following you. Your snooping around has been getting on my nerves. I don't see why you had to stick your nose where it doesn't belong." She emphasized her words by shaking the gun at me. "If the police couldn't solve it what made you think you could?"

For a millisecond I was confused, then realized she wasn't talking about our teacher's death. She had to be talking about the other murder. I forgot myself, and blurted, "You were involved in the Bobby Lee Ghoston murder?"

From her wild-eyed response, I knew I'd hit a nerve. "Don't play dumb with me, Tracie"

"It's Trixie." Stupid, don't correct her. What does it matter anyway with a gun barrel up your nostril?

"How would you like it if your daddy denied you?"

"Bobby was your father?" Wow, I didn't see that one coming. I thought she killed Annie, but couldn't tie the two murders together. Until now.

Amanda's face softened for a minute. "Yes." The gun lowered just a hair. I thought she might put it down, but it shot right back up. "After years of begging my mother to tell me who my real father was, she finally broke. I confronted Bobby Lee with the news and he laughed. Can you believe that? He laughed and asked how I could be so sure since my mother had so many lovers."

I tried disarming her by showing her sympathy. "That must have been very hurtful, Amanda."

She glared at me, nostrils flaring. This girl had some real trust issues. "How would you know how I felt? How dare he? I knew my mother wasn't lying. It was okay for him to take in that Tabitha girl who wasn't even kin to him and raise her like a daughter, but why couldn't he acknowledge me? Well I wasn't going to let him get away with it." She swung the gun around like a conductor's baton.

Dear Lord, please keep me safe and give me the wisdom to get out of here alive. A light bulb turned on and I fought my shaking hands. If she'd shot Tippi, she was on a murdering rampage and what was one more body on her long list?

"A jury isn't going to blame you." I glanced around the room for a path of escape. There wasn't one. Amanda was standing between me and the door. "You've had such a rough time, they'll understand, I just know it." Then I recalled the recorder in my pocket. If I could switch it on without her knowing, I could get a confession and perhaps solve my own murder post mortem.

"You're just saying that to get me off your back." Amanda wiped a tear, turning aside to keep me from seeing it.

"No, I'm not. I have a tissue for that. I'm just going to reach into my coat pocket." I held up a hand the way I'd seen in the shows. "See? Just going for a tissue. You know I don't carry a gun anyway." I slid my hand in, found the recorder and hoped I'd switched it to record, not erase. Then I found a used Kleenex. "Here you go."

She took the tissue and dabbed at her streaked face.

"Now, why not tell me everything? I have some connections with the police, and I may be able to help."

"Why should I trust you?" She shoved the tissue in her jeans pocket and two-fisted the gun in my face again.

"Who else *can* you trust?" I thought quickly. "I have a daughter about your age, and I think I know how you must feel. Her father wasn't the best example in the world either."

"Oh?"

I told her about Jill's dad, and may have embellished the facts a little to give Amanda's nervous energy a chance to subside. "So, tell me. How did I frighten you when I mentioned looking into the Ghoston murder, and how is Tippi involved?" Speak into the microphone, there's a good killer.

"You mean, Tabitha?" She spit out the name like it was venom. "I discovered she was attending the class and decided this was my chance. When I saw her driving that little red sports car and wearing those fancy clothes it just got under my craw. I should've been the one to inherit all that money. I thought if I got rid of her then I could claim my inheritance."

I glanced at my watch. It had only been twenty minutes since I'd left

Nana and Dee Dee. Would they figure out something happened when I didn't show up at our appointed time? I had to keep Amanda talking until I could come up with a plan? I had to try.

"Why Annie?"

A cloud passed over her face. "That was stupid Ladonna's fault. I heard her say she was going to deliver tea service, and thought she was going to Tabitha's, so I laced the pot when she wasn't looking. But she went to Annie's room first, and it was too late for me to stop her."

"So you had to frame someone for spiking the tea, and picked me?"

She nodded. "If I framed you, then you'd be out of the way and couldn't continue researching Bobby Lee's murder. It was easy when I found some of her favorite tea in the kitchen."

I was beginning to feel a bit light-headed, and was growing a raging headache. "That was some brilliant detective work on your part. What with the poison and framing me and all."

She seemed to grow a bit taller. "Rhododendrons. My ex-scumbag of a husband works for a landscaper. At least he was good for something. Taught me which common household plants are poisonous."

Somewhere a pipe moaned, and the building shifted. The spell was broken. Startled, Amanda turned toward the noise. I didn't give it a second thought. I karate chopped her hand and the gun flew across the floor. She dove for it, and I ran.

CHAPTER THIRTY-FIVE

I hid behind a brown paper covered canvas. My heart beat faster than a hummingbird's wings. I feared Amanda could hear it. "I know you're back there, Trixie. You can't hide forever." When she walked past me, I took the opportunity to escape to another hiding place. This time I hid behind a Rubenesque statue. She kinda reminded me of Dee Dee.

I grabbed my phone to text Dee, but remembered the beeps would give me away. I glanced at my watch and saw forty minutes had passed.

"I know what you've been doing. You might as well come on out and get it over with."

Yeah, sure. I didn't come out of hiding, no way, but my knees shook so hard I bumped into Dee Dee's twin and gave away my hidey-hole. Amanda came at me like the crazed woman she was. We struggled over the gun. I found my inner strength, grabbed her hair and jerked her head back to get her in a firm head lock. She let out a scream loud enough to wake the dead.

At that moment, the elevator doors burst open and out came the police, followed by Dee and Nana. The cavalry had arrived just in time.

It was wonderful to be back at Mama's, sitting around the fireplace with the people I loved most: Nana, Dee Dee, her daughter Stephanie, and my daughter Jill and of course my beloved Beau. We'd just eaten a traditional Christmas dinner of turkey and dressing, green beans, mashed potatoes, and all the trimmings. When we thought we couldn't eat any more, we found room for a slice of red velvet, or german chocolate cake.

Nana had everyone's attention as she repeated the story for the hundredth time. "You should have seen us. Dee Dee and I were looking through the telescope when we saw Amanda on the deck with your mama. We jumped up and down and waved, but we couldn't get her attention." She turned toward Dee Dee for affirmation as if we didn't believe her. "Isn't that right, Dee?"

"It sure is. And that's when we called 911 and told them to let Detective Sams know Amanda had Trixie."

"Yeah, and we knew they were in the mansion, we just didn't know where. The police set up a floor by floor search, and we finally made it to the basement just in time."

"That would be when I grabbed Amanda by the hair," I said. "What I still don't recall is how I got this tremendous pain in the back of my head."

Amanda had fought back, and as I worked to disarm her, she flailed at me. She might have scrambled my brains a bit, but she didn't dislodge the recorder that caught the whole thing.

Now Amanda was going to be a guest of the government for a very long time, and it wasn't going to be in any mansion.

"I'm just grateful to be alive. She was on a murder spree and I was almost her next victim. She murdered Bobby Lee Ghoston because he denied she was his daughter. When she found out I was on the trail she decided to get rid of me, too. She killed Annie and framed me. As if this wasn't enough murder and mayhem she tried to kill Tippi hoping she'd be able to claim her inheritance."

I snuggled up against my Beau. I was never so glad to see anyone when he flew home right away after Dee Dee called and told him we'd caught Amanda and I was being treated at Erlanger for my war wound.

"Well, I'm thankful you're all in one piece," Beau said. Nana sat on the other side of Beau. He reached over and gave her a shoulder hug.

"And that goes for you and Dee Dee, too. I sure don't want to lose my favorite girls." Nana turned cherry red.

I settled in to watch the flames flicker up the chimney, happy we were all together, now. Harv couldn't have been more pleased to have another article to publish about a solved case. My feature about Bobby Lee Ghoston and the Dixie Mafia was selling lots of copies of *Georgia by the Way*. Tippi a.k.a. Tabitha was thrilled I'd ask her to contribute, and I was more than glad to give her credit.

"Enough shop talk about murders and evidence and proper police procedures." Beau looked down at me. "Now what's this I hear about you being the champion spitter of Chattanooga?"

I felt my face glowing warmer than the yule log, and I cut a look at Nana. "Thanks a lot!"

They all broke out in laughter, and I held a hand to my bandaged head, and laughed right along with them.

tion can be obtained
ing.com
SA
423
2B/76

CPSIA information can be obtained
at www.ICGtesting.com
Printed in the USA
JSHW021959180423
40531JS00002B/76